For Alex . . . who's held my hand ever so tightly over the years, never letting go in the red-rover game of life. I love you.

Dogs are better than human beings
because they know but do not tell.

—*Emily Dickinson*

OLIVIA SAMMS

SNITCH

THE BEA CATCHER CHRONICLES: BOOK 2

SKYSCAPE

SKYSCAPE

This is a work of fiction. Names, characters, organizations, places, events, and incidents are either products of the author's imagination or are used fictitiously.

Text copyright © 2014 Olivia Samms
All rights reserved.

Published by Skyscape, New York

www.apub.com

Amazon, the Amazon logo, and Skyscape are trademarks of Amazon.com, Inc., or its affiliates.

ISBN-13: 9781477847237
ISBN-10: 1477847235

Book design by Sammy Yuen and Susan Gerber

Printed in the United States of America

Joshua had known where he was going to do it, and how he was going to do it, but had to wait for the spring thaw, after the harsh, icy winter in Ann Arbor, Michigan.

A senior at Chelsea High School, he had been surprised by the unexpected Christmas present from his girlfriend, Tina. "I'm preggers, Josh," she had told him between hot and heavy breaths as they parked in front of a nativity scene at the United Church of Christ.

So, on the first day of the spring season, when Gallup Park began renting out canoes on the Huron River, Joshua skipped his afternoon classes, making sure that he and Tina were one of the first to rent out a yellow fiberglass vessel.

He hummed to himself as they paddled around the calm, murky water, passing under the shade of tall cedars that lined the muddy banks—their oars in sync, dodging spiky reeds, dipping swans, and quacking ducks delirious with the warming waters.

Joshua eventually anchored the boat under a great weeping willow—a tree that Tina thought looked like a waterfall with its delicate branches draping, hanging so low they tickled the tops of their heads.

He placed his wooden oar carefully inside the canoe, reached into his fleece-lined parka, pulled out a purple velvet box, and awkwardly knelt. The boat rocked, prompting Tina to hold tightly to the sides, giggling. "Josh, no, you didn't, did you? Is this what today was all about?"

Joshua's smile gave it all away. There was nothing else to say but "Tina, I love you. Will you marry me?" She gasped. Her hand covered her mouth, her head shook back and forth as she cried, "Oh my god, no. No. No . . ."

"What? You're saying no? Are you kidding me?"

She continued her wide-eyed whimpering as Joshua sank back down on his butt. He contemplated jumping into the water and pocketed the ring box. "You could've let on, Tina. I mean, for chris-sakes. You saw the receipt; I know you did."

Tina said nothing—only lifted her hand off her mouth and pointed a trembling finger toward the muddy bank, her face set in a silent, horrified scream.

At first he thought it was a rotted, waterlogged tree trunk as it bobbed around in the white, foamy waves at the edge of the river.

A school of fish rushed in and surrounded it, until a larger small-mouthed bass shooed them away, circled, and nibbled at the bloated body as it rolled up onto the mucky shore—a young African American teen, fully clothed. His wide-open eyes fixed on Joshua and

Tina straight on, as if he were the one surprised by the encounter. A diamond stud in the lobe of his ear, much bigger than the one in Josh's pocket, sparkled, mocking them.

Josh jumped. The canoe rocked sharply to the right. He tried to correct the jolt, jerking his body hard, port side, and the oars fell out first. Then the boat wobbled, picked up momentum, and flipped over, creating a wake, and dumping him and Tina into the dark, inky water.

He frantically dog-paddled to Tina, then felt something at his back, and turned. . . . The body was now beside him. A finger—gray, wrinkled, and shriveled like a clump of upchucked cat fur—tapped at his cheek.

He texted me late last night. Told me to meet him at 7 a.m. at our usual place.

I wake early (having barely slept) and scribble out a note—a lie—for the parents, leaving it tucked under the coffeemaker before I fly out the door:

> Hitting the sunrise AA meeting at St. Anne's before school. Luv, Bea

I park on a quiet residential street nearby in Ypsilanti, at the corner of River and Maple, as instructed; get out of my car; and quietly close the door, hoping not to draw any attention to myself. But a friggin' bird lands on the hood of my car and starts chirping its little beak off—different melodies and really loud for its size. I shush it but must remind it of another song 'cause it flies away, singing a new rendition, in a different key, and even louder.

I hurry along the sidewalk and startle at a sprinkler spurting on. The smell of wet grass fills my nostrils, and I stifle a sneeze. My spring allergies are on high alert with all the flowers and shit blooming—sinuses spazzing, forcing me to take my nose ring out. And my eyes are all red and swollen from itching. The mascara that I carefully applied this morning is, I'm sure, smeared. *Damn*, I wanted to look hot for him.

My pulse quickens, as it always does, knowing that within minutes I'll see him, get my fix, and feel that buzzy *zing* race through me like an electrical current.

I start to jog and then immediately slow my pace as an elderly woman steps out the front door of her house to collect the newspaper from the lawn. Not expecting to see me—or anyone for that matter, I'm guessing, as she is dressed in a pink baby doll nightie—she stops mid-bend and freezes as if she were a lawn statue.

I kind of do a little wave and smile. She grunts, swiftly tucking the paper under her arm, and scuttles off into her house, pulling the bottom of the ruffled hem down over her ass. *You go, girl!*

The white eyelet curtain on the windowed door opens a smidgen, as she spies on the suspicious black girl walking on her street early in the morning.

I don't want her calling the police, the neighborhood watch, or to be followed—he'd be pissed—so I'll just act like I'm out for a brisk morning walk. I raise my arms up and lean over, touching my toes, stretching out my very tight—*ow*—hamstrings, and peek between my legs, noticing that the curtain is now closed. I stand back up, get a little dizzy with the rush in my head, when my damn phone rings—I forgot to set it to vibrate—and I frantically dig it out of the bottom of my bag.

It's my best friend, Chris Mayes:

Me (I whisper): Wazzup?
Chris: I need you to draw Ian.
Me: What?
Chris: Draw the truth out of him. I don't know if he's
    into me anymore.
Me: Chris, I don't really have time for this.
Chris: But I should be able to use you—your power.

I trip while rushing across the railroad tracks at Depot Town, fumble the phone, almost dropping it.

Chris: Where are you, anyway? You sound out of breath.
Me: I woke up late—trying to get ready for school.

The stupid bird is evidently following me, singing another song from the maple tree above.

Chris: Since when do you have a bird?

I give it the evil eye; it works, and the bird flies away.

Me: I gotta go. See you first period?
Chris: Fine.

He hangs up in a huff.

I hate lying to him and don't know how long I can keep up the sham. But I can't tell him about the secret meetings. . . . He'd never understand.

I grab on to the budding birch trees as I carefully hike the steep ravine that heads down toward the river. The sun shines brightly through the cedars that drape the gully. I stifle another sneeze, hoping not to wake the sleeping homeless person that lives in a cardboard refrigerator box. I happened upon him once before—he was nice and all, but he scared the shit out of me. He politely asked if I could spare some change. I gave him a five—the only bill I could find in my bag. He seemed grateful, and I think because of my generosity he ignores my occasional hookups here with *him*—but I'm sure I'll be hit up for more money soon.

I wrap my long, crocheted ecru sweater coat around my body and scoot along a rickety wooden bridge; climb a wet, grassy hill (dampening the bottom hem of my flared bell-bottom jeans and soaking my fringed moccasin sandals); and reach the abandoned, more than 150-year-old original City Hall in downtown Ypsilanti, Michigan, six miles southeast of

Ann Arbor. The stone squat building sits nestled in a woody thicket, bordering the Huron River.

I crawl through a boarded-up window in the back. Scaffolding leans against the crumbling plaster of the graffiti-covered walls. Yellowed, torn architecture plans lie scattered on the wide, wood-planked floors. In the corner, a chained-off spiral staircase leads to an old jail cell. And he's there, sitting on a high-backed bench in the middle of the room, looking a little peeved.

"You're late."

"I'm sorry."

"Did anyone see you?"

"Just an old lady, but I think she's more concerned about *me* seeing her—the way she looked."

"You sure?"

"Yeah, I'm sure. Chill." I take a step toward him. "You said you got something for me?"

He nods, pats the bench, gesturing for me to join him.

I do, and I am hit, walloped with his smell—a woodsy, spicy, eucalyptus-y smell—and my sinuses clear; my tummy, as always, does a flip-floppy thing.

Sergeant Dan Daniels from the Ann Arbor Police Department stands, paces. He's wearing a light brown Windbreaker over faded Levi's—frayed, ripped, worn through in places down to his skin. Jeans that have probably grown with him over the years, scarred with life's experiences. And being in the police force for nearly a decade, working himself up the ranks rapidly to sergeant—ever since he was out of high school—he, too, is worn in places.

"I got a case for you. It's troubling me. Dealing with a kid your age."

"I'm not a kid. I'm almost eighteen." I check the timer app on my phone and flaunt it in his face. "It says here, it's only six days, sixteen hours, and forty-five minutes till my birthday."

"Yeah, yeah, right. Sorry." He scratches the blond sandpaper beard on his cheeks and chin. "Well, anyway, this guy, he's just seventeen."

"So, what did he do?"

"My theory? A lot less than what he's copping to. I'm questioning him at the station this afternoon." He stops. Looks at me. "You think you could help me out?"

I jump up. "Oh my god. You're messin' with me, right? You want me to do my thing at the police station?"

He blows through his lips, sits back down on the bench, and leans forward with his elbows on his knees. Shakes his head no, but then says, "Yeah, I do. It's crazy, but I do."

"This is so cool." I lift my fringed suede bag up and over my shoulder and sit cross-legged on the floor, barely able to contain the revved-up feeling that motors through me.

"His name is Junior. A senior at Skyline High."

"The high school across town."

"Yeah."

I take my Moleskine out of my purse—a sketchbook that I am never without—turn to a clean page to take notes, grab the pen that's tucked behind my ear. It catches on a curl—pulls. "Ouch."

I never should have had my mom cut it last fall—long story why: my hair is half Afro frizz from my dad's side, half a thick, tangled Italian mess from my mom's. It was great at first, having it short—freeing—and it was so easy in the morning not having to think about it. But I wasn't totally down with how I looked. I like variation, changing things up. So I'm growing it out now. My curls aren't tight enough for a classic 'fro—the four inches or so (of mayhem) sort of flops flat, like ungroomed poodle fur, parted in the middle.

The only product that keeps my hair in control—less frizzy and super shiny—is olive oil. In particular, my mom's expensive imported virgin oil. (And, oh my god, if she found out, she'd kill me.) She's not a cook—far from it—but I think the oil somehow keeps her connected to her Italian roots (not talking hair here), and she sprinkles it on everything as if blessing it. I've been sneaking the oil into a spritz bottle. So far she hasn't noticed—fingers crossed, because you don't want to tap into my mom's fiery temper, for sure.

I finally get the pen detangled, ready to take notes, and look up into his Caribbean Sea green eyes.

"This one's tricky, Bea. Maybe you'll be able to get something out of him. We've had an undercover at the school for a couple weeks now, suspecting some major dealing going on.

He did a random bag check after school yesterday when the teams were practicing and found a few pounds of brick weed stashed in this kid's gym bag."

I swallow. "Whoa. That's not just an afternoon high. Sounds like a dealer to me."

"Yeah, but he has no priors, squeaky clean from what we've found out. He was basically looking at a misdemeanor until Cole started digging around, asking him questions."

"Detective Cole? Your partner, that doofus pig?"

"Bea. I'm a police sergeant. You don't say *pig* in front of me."

I laugh. "You didn't object to the *doofus* part. Tell me something . . . does Junior still have his fingernails?"

"Cole didn't torture him."

"You sure about that? What does he look like? Is he black?"

He nods.

"Then of course Detective Cole thinks he's guilty." I finger twist my hair.

"Stop that," he scolds. "He's a good cop."

"Not from what I've seen. And would you doubt these? Huh?" I point at my eyes, open them wide, teasing the Sarge.

Daniels stands—turns away. "Don't you dare, Bea."

"Don't I dare what?"

"Draw me—what I'm thinking about."

"I wasn't. Jeez." But I was. I'd already put it down on the page—a rough sketch. It flashed in front of me like a neon sign as I studied him: my eyes. I saw my eyes in his, as if I were staring into a mirror. My almond-shaped, kohl-lined, mascara-smeared hazel eyes.

He likes me. I know he really likes me, and it's mind-blowing, stupid crazy weird—the thought of the two of us together. He's a cop, twenty-eight, and I'm a seventeen-year-old (almost eighteen) recovering addict who spent a substantial amount of time running from the police. We shouldn't even be thinking of each other in *that way*, and we haven't done anything about it—haven't even admitted it . . . yet.

But one thing I've learned in the past year is to give up all the *shoulds* and *shouldn'ts*. The "you-*should*-do-this" and "you-*shouldn't*-do-that" crap: graduate high school, go to college, meet a frat boy, get married, and have a family. Yeah, I think a lot of peeps live by the *shoulds* on the outside, but not on the inside.

On the inside it's all about secrets and lies.

"Back to the case." He grumbles and sits on the bench, avoiding eye contact. "I need you to draw the truth out of him."

"Well, like . . . duh."

He chuckles.

I love getting him to laugh. He's so serious all the time, his blond, fluffy caterpillar eyebrows always pushed together with grown-up worry. But the humor fizzles away—it lasts a second, and he rubs his big paws together. "We pulled a body out of the Huron Monday."

I slam my sketchbook shut.

"A teen—troubled . . . in and out of gangs. His name was Jamal. Classmate of Junior's. Was shot dead and then dumped."

I shiver. "Holy crap, that's gruesome."

"Yeah, I know. So here's this kid, Junior, denying the pot was his, insisting he didn't know where it came from, why it was in his bag, when Detective Cole brings up what happened to Jamal. He asked Junior if he knew anything about it, and then, out of the blue, Junior suddenly changes his mind and confesses—says yeah, the weed was his. He's been dealing, and—get this . . . he says he killed Jamal."

I sit up straighter.

"Said he tossed the murder weapon, the gun, in the river along with the body." Daniels massages his temples. "So there you have it. The evidence is somewhere at the bottom of the Huron—a 130-mile-long river. Not easy to prove, and he knows it."

"Why do you have to prove it? He confessed."

"Yeah, that's what Cole says."

Damn. Not cool, me thinking like Detective Cole.

The sergeant walks over to the stairs and jingles the rusty chain.

I've been tempted to venture down those steps. Evidently the old jail cell leads to one of a series of tunnels that runs under the Huron. The tunnels were originally built for drainage, but urban legend has it that escaped slaves from the south hid in them. They'd wait till night, and then in the darkness, board boats that took them down river, eventually escaping to Canada. But now the tunnels, when not flooded, house taggers, drug dealers, and ballsy teens. . . . I wouldn't have hesitated to explore them a year ago.

"It doesn't add up," Daniels continues. "We confiscated his cell phone. Talked to his teachers, the pastor at the church where he sings in a choir, and we came up with nothing. He's a good student, good kid."

"You know as well as I—I'm living proof. Sometimes bad shit happens to—"

"Good people. I know. But this isn't the case. I think someone set Junior up. Planted the drugs. Knew there was a narc in the school . . ."

"What makes you think that?"

"It was just too easy. An unzipped Nike bag sitting on a bench in the locker room, saying, *Hey, look at me. Look what I'm carrying.* No one's that stupid. And then the sudden confession? Doesn't make sense. He's considered an adult here in Michigan—first-degree murder—life in state prison."

"So . . . you have any ideas? Who would set him up, and why he confessed?"

He shakes his head. "We checked out his family—most of them are up to no good. A lot of gang activity going on in the house, around their 'hood, and where there's smoke, there's—"

"Someone getting fucked up."

"This is serious, Bea. Junior knows something, is covering for someone—but he's not talking."

"It doesn't make any sense that he'd take the heat for someone else."

"That's what I need you to find out." He walks back to the bench and sits. "Listen to me; this could be dangerous. Drugs involved. You sure you're up to it?"

"Are you kidding me? This is badass shit. I'm in."

The sergeant leans forward on the bench, clasps his hands. "Okay. I'm going to have to figure something out, like how to sneak you in the station without raising any eyebrows. Especially with Detective Cole around."

"Yeah, that jerk hates me."

"No, he doesn't. He's just suspicious of you—doesn't understand . . . the thing you do." Daniels laughs. "But then again, why would he?"

"I still say he hates me." I stand and brush the dust off my butt. "Why don't you arrest me for something?"

"What?"

"I know how to be sketchy. Pull me in like I'm one of the bad guys."

He stands, rubs his furry brow. "I don't know about that."

"What time are you thinking?" I pop open the calendar on my phone.

"I'll need you about four."

"Great. It'll give me time to get ready. I should have a look going on."

He rolls his eyes. "Bea, you don't need a look. This isn't a game; we don't need to pretend anything."

"Of course we do." I check the time on my phone. "Whoa, it's getting late. I'd better get to school for first period. I already have a few tardies and sure don't want the office to call and freak out my parents."

He crosses over to the exit window and pushes the plywood board—gives the go-ahead. "It's clear."

I crawl through the window and jump down onto the matted brown grass below.

Daniels follows but struggles, squeezing his more than six-foot frame through the narrow window—one long, lanky leg sticks out, feeling for the ground, followed by the other, then his torso. He ducks his head, but catches the top of his blond hair on the ragged edge of the sill. And then swears.

I can't help but laugh.

He boards up the window, straightens his hair, and brushes off his clothes. "Come to the back door on Fifth Street at four. I'll take it from there."

"'K. See you then." I salute him.

"Stop with the shit, Bea."

"But I wouldn't be me, would I? Without the shit. By the way . . . your fly's open."

His face instantly reddens as he looks down at the zipped-up crotch of his pants.

"Happy April Fool's Day, Dan Daniels." I climb down the hill, pass the refrigerator box (the homeless guy now stirring), and scamper through the gully. And I know that the Sarge will wait, looking after me—give it roughly three minutes and then he'll follow, making sure I drive off safely.

I sometimes slow my pace and listen for his heavy footsteps clunking across the bridge, sense his presence, his eyes watching me, warming my back, guiding me to my car.

I plop down my bag on the passenger seat, look at the time, take out my Moleskine, and write:

> 6 days, 16 hours, and 5 minutes till I'm 18. ☺ I can't wait! No one can tell me what I should do, who I should see . . . I'll finally be an adult!

I study the sketched eyes on the page—what I drew when I looked at him—what he was thinking about. Me. My eyes.

It still wigs me out—this bizarre skill I have—the skill that Sergeant Daniels calls me in for. Pen in hand, paper in front of me, when studying someone, an image may come charging through my head like a wild stallion—galloping, kicking dirt up in my face. Sometimes it tickles as a feather would, fluttering in and out like a daydream. And sometimes what I see hits me hard, like an anvil crushing down, and my head pounds for hours afterward. As the image appears, it possesses me—possesses my right hand, and I sketch it down on paper.

I can draw the truth out of people . . . literally.

This whacked-out, freaky power happened when I got

sober—the first time—nine months ago in rehab. It was like I was airing out my brain, freeing it from the drugs and making room for the wicked insight into what others were thinking— and some of it was not so cool.

Last fall, Sergeant Daniels didn't believe me when I saw and drew the truth out of Willa Pressman, the most popular girl in our senior class. I sketched the face of the man who raped her—a serial killer. Daniels thought I was full of it until the creep was positively ID'd by Willa herself.

Now he calls me in to our secret place whenever he needs my assistance. That's the only positive thing about my skill: I help Sergeant Daniels catch bad guys. I guess you could say that I'm a paranormal forensic artist.

Weird, right?

The first time he used me was right before Christmas. I was asked to park my butt in the middle of the local mall and draw Santa Claus. Daniels had an inkling that the recent wave of shoplifting had something to do with the man in the red suit.

Excited for the challenge, I made a trip to my favorite vintage clothing shop. Leila, the owner, rocks, big time. She haunts estate sales, trolls eBay, and pulls in the trippiest shit, and at a bargain-basement price. I don't know the last time I bought something new.

I had picked out a bloodred, velvet eighties blazer—with two-inch shoulder pads that could compete with any fullback on the Detroit Lions. I wore it with black leggings and my over-the-knee, "don't fuck with me" leather boots. And keeping in the spirit of things, I festively combed a sprig of holly in my then very short, cropped hair.

A long line of children wrapped around the giant, tinsel-draped fake fir tree. At first I was only picking up images from the kids: toys, action figures, dolls, train sets flooded my mind and filled the pages of my sketchbook.

But then, staring into Santa's beady blue eyes, it hit me—hard. *Bam.* Mr. Claus was thinking about a little boutique jewelry store on the second floor of the mall, focusing on a silver-beaded clutch purse in the window—the one I had drooled over a month ago but couldn't afford. This was one of those headache images (a headache that took two days to get rid of). I guess hearing for the second time in my life that Old Kriss Kringle was a phony set the migraine off.

I texted the Sarge, tipping him off, and Santa's break was interrupted as he attempted to tuck the sixty-dollar clutch into his black patent leather, silver-buckled belt. He was quietly and calmly taken aside and arrested; and I'm sure Mrs. Claus must have been disappointed, because the clutch went back to the window display.

The other case I helped crack involved insurance fraud. The image of water *whooshed*, flooding through me when I searched a plastic surgeon assistant's eyes—cascaded down like a water-fall. Sergeant Daniels pressed her with this information, and she caved—blurted it all out. Her boss was hiding away in an Upper Peninsula cabin near the Tahquamenon Falls (they were bonking each other, too).

But today is a first. . . . In the police station. Wow.

6 days
15 hours
55 minutes

pull my rusted-out, kick-ass Volvo sedan into the parking lot. I'm in my second semester of my senior year at the local public school, Packard High. The name is appropriate, because it's packed with over two thousand (mostly) high students. I've been here ever since I was expelled from a very elite private school, Athena Day School for Girls, because of my gnarly drug problem (and a messy incident at a rave in Detroit last summer). I was thrown into rehab for three months and then deposited here, at Packrat High—as Chris calls it.

I really don't want to do this high school thing anymore—get up every morning and deal with another day of the *shoulds*. I'm *so* done and have no idea how I'm going to trudge through the bullshit sludge of the next month and a half. I wish it were just senioritis. But I know it's not. It's an 'itis, for sure, though—malignant, doesn't have a cure—and is spreading fast through my body.

I free-fall into a fit of sneezing, my car swerves, and I almost wipe out a gaggle of geeky freshmen from the birdwatcher's club. They appropriately flip me the bird. I wave an apology. "Sorry, didn't mean to almost kill you."

Damn. My nose won't stop running. I feel for the box of Kleenex sitting next to me, shotgun. The box is empty. I dart my eyes at all the junk in the backseat. My car has been sort of a mobile locker for the last year—school stuff, odds and ends, and half my closet lives back there. I rustle through books, papers, a pair of jeans that are way too big for me (I cuff them high on my shins and cinch them around my waist when I'm feeling a bloated day coming on), empty Styrofoam coffee cups, Chris's extra-large hoodie, red high-top sneakers that look wicked good with my shredded jean miniskirt—but I can't find a tissue. I get my hand around a roll of toilet paper—try to remember why it's there . . . actually, on second thought, don't want to—and tear off a few squares, roll the end of the tissue into a ball, and stick it up my nostril—shove it in like a tampon. Not a pretty sight, but it does the trick, and then I park in the designated senior lot.

Chris is standing behind his car, madly sucking face with his boyfriend, Ian, a junior, and, LOL, the guy he wants me to draw because he's afraid he *isn't into him* anymore.

Chris jumps as I toot my horn, and he smooths the long side of his hair. He was there, holding my hand, supporting me when I decided to let my mom buzz me last fall—again, long story—so he decided to let her cut his. But he chickened out mid-buzz, so baby-fine, bleach-blond hair hangs straight, tucked behind one ear, and the other side he keeps short.

I roll down my window (yes, roll . . . that's how old the car is). "Jesus, get a room, you two," I joke.

"What the hell is up your nose?" Chris asks, lifting the camera that hangs around his neck—always (he wears it like an accessory, and is an awesome photographer)—and snaps a picture.

"Toilet paper."

"Hah," he mocks. "I knew you were full of shit."

I stick my tongue out at him, and he shoots another pic.

Ian's red bangs fall down into his freckled face—his blue eyes are thinly lined with black. "You guys act like you're two."

"Do not," I say.

"Do too," Chris parries.

"Nice Guyliner, Ian," I say.

He punches Chris's shoulder. "Told you it looked good."

"What does she know?" Chris says.

I get in his face and cross my eyes. "Everything, you moron."

Click, click. "Yeah . . . full of shit, like I said." He leans in, whispers, "I don't know . . . what do you think—is Ian acting different?"

"Stop being so paranoid, dude," I whisper back.

"Dang. I love those bell-bottoms you have on, Bea," Ian says as we walk toward the school.

"Yeah, they're so wide, you could hide small children under them." Chris laughs.

"Groovy, aren't they? Vintage sixties—from Leila's place." I remove the snot-ridden clump from my nose and toss it in the trash. "Damn these allergies. To hell with those bees and their sex lives."

"Speaking of a Bea's sex life, how's Wendell?" Chris nudges me.

I sigh. "I don't know. I don't seem to be ready for that yet."

"Are you kidding me? He's like a god." Ian fans himself. Chris's brow furrows.

"He is, isn't he?" I shrug my shoulders. "It's weird—but it doesn't feel . . . right. Not with him at least." I mumble the last part.

"I heard that. What do you mean *at least*? You got someone else goin' on? Let me see your phone." He shoves his hand in my purse.

"Stop it." I slap him away.

"Why? What's on it that you don't want me to see—who've you called, huh?"

"Nobody." I can't help smiling. But, I don't want him to see the texts from Sergeant Daniels.

The bell rings on the prison yard, and students scurry out of their cars, from behind cinder-block walls, up from the bleachers in the football stadium, out of parked school buses. Clouds of cigarette and marijuana smoke hover, dissipate, floating up into the sky as they approach the sprawling redbrick walls of higher learning . . . *not*.

I wave and mouth *hi* at the security camera tucked away

on the ceiling as we enter the heavy metal doors. Principal Nathanson monitors the camera every morning like an SS guard. Who knows what he's scanning for or what he'd do if he actually saw someone smuggling something bad in the school. I could be hiding a couple bricks of weed under the bells of my bottoms, and he wouldn't have a clue.

"I'll see you at lunch?" Chris pinches Ian's ass.

"If you're lucky." Ian winks and walks off.

Chris bites his knuckles. "God, I love him so much it hurts. Who do you think he's into?"

"*You*, you idiot. You were all over each other in the parking lot, sheesh." I open my locker and brace myself for the crap that will undoubtedly fall out.

Books, shoes, art supplies, and my crumpled PE T-shirt tumble toward me. "Oh, cool. I was looking for that." I toss the tee into my bag, shove the rest of the shit back in my locker, and slam it shut. "The coach said I'd get a detention if I forgot my uniform again."

"How the hell do you know where anything is, Bea?"

"I don't. I've given up trying to control things. I figure if it's meant to be in my life, it'll surface somehow, right?" I wipe my runny nose on the sleeve of my sweater.

"Bea! Chris!" Willa Pressman, wearing her cheerleading uniform, prances up to us, her sleek, blond ponytail swaying back and forth like a palomino's tail.

"Hey, Willa."

She gives me a once-over, scans me up and down like I'm a

bar code, then pulls a compact box of tissues out of her purse and hands it to me.

"See, Chris? Meant to be." I blow my nose. "Allergies," I say to Willa.

She then pulls out a large bottle of hand sanitizer from her rolling backpack, obviously not believing me. "You should keep this on you at all times." And then she gives me a European air-kiss on both cheeks. It's a greeting all the cheerleaders have adopted, and weirdly, somehow, I've been included in the ritual—accepted in the pack, whether I like it or not. Very odd—me being a part of the rah-rah crowd. I've always been an outcast, made fun of by those types. But Willa accepted me into her world, and that meant everybody else has to, because she's, like, the school rock star.

Got to give props to her, though, because rock star or not, Willa went through hell and back last fall, surviving the brutal beating and rape in September and kicking a wicked drug and alcohol problem in the butt (she's been sober almost six months—a little longer than me). Now she flits around the school, organizes dances, manages clubs, and tirelessly works every week on a rape hotline. It's hard to keep up with her.

The rest of the uniformed pack approaches.

"Hi, Bea." Sarah waves a curled pinky. "Mwaa." Air-kiss #2 for the day.

"Hey, girlfriend." Eva Marie hip-butts me. Air kiss #3.

The girls finish their mimed greetings (very sanitary, if you think about it) and hand Willa the floor. "Listen up. A special person is turning eighteen next week . . ."

Oh no, she remembered. Please, Willa, don't make a big deal. But why am I surprised? She probably has the birth date of every person in the whole school neatly filed away in the contact app on her phone. All eyes are now on me, and I'm expecting a piñata or disco ball to break through the heavens and descend upon us.

Instead, Willa's asshole boyfriend, Zac—unfortunately my neighbor—joins us, leans against a locker, and pulls her in, wrapping his thick, hairy arms around her waist.

He's King Jock Itch here at Packard High—the star wrestler, with season record-breaking pins. Full of BS, he somehow successfully pins down teachers and Principal Nathanson, talking them into passing grades with a wink and a flex, and, unbelievably, he aced the SAT—a nearly perfect score. He won't shut up about it.

"What are you all talking about, huh?" Zac's smile disappears when he sees that I'm part of the crowd. And then his jaw does this weird twitchy thing—seems to happen whenever he sees me. It spasms like an imaginary tie is tightening around his neck.

"Your SAT score, of course." Chris falsely swoons. "What else is there to talk about?"

"Fuck off, dweeb." Zac flicks the words out at Chris like he's toe fungus.

"That's enough, you two." Willa stands on tiptoe and kisses Zac on the cheek. "We were talking about Bea's birthday, and I was thinking we could pull together a little party . . ."

"No, really, Willa, that isn't necessary," I mutter.

"Of course it is." She checks the calendar on her phone, flipping her finger through dates as if she's conducting the string section of an orchestra . . . up-tempo. "I have the evening of the seventh free. That would be the day before your birthday, but you wouldn't mind that, would you, Bea?"

"Uh, I think I have plans that day," Zac, the jerk, spits out.

"Oh, well, maybe another day, then . . . ," she says, her calendar closed, eyes on Zac.

This is so not cool. Truthfully? I wanted to enjoy the fuss over the planning, the stress of it all for just a second, at least, so I could say no, try and talk Willa out of it, complain to Chris, and then despair for days over what I should wear.

I love Willa. Really, I do. But her choice in men? Majorly flawed—big time. Unfortunately, boyfriends seem to be her new drug of choice, and she has absolutely no bullshit radar.

Last semester, when she was stoned out of her mind, she dated the captain of the football team, Jackass Jones. (Okay, I added the ass part, but he was—and still is.) By the time Willa came back to school from rehab, he was dating skanky Scarlett Ross. Willa pretended it didn't hurt her feelings and bought them a Hallmark card congratulating them on their relationship.

Personally, I would have castrated the guy. Come to think

of it, Jack has been kind of castrated, at least online. He was defriended by almost everybody. But the next week? Willa was *in love* with Rob. *Bea, he's so dreamy, he's the greatest.* That lasted only about two weeks, before she moved on to my jerky neighbor.

"Come on, Willa, let's go," Zac demands, pulling her arm.

"We're going to be late for art class, you guys," Eva Marie says, scooting down the hall.

"I'm going to have to miss it. There's a special student council meeting." Willa gazes proudly at Zac. "Tell them what you're doing, babe."

"Um, I'm talking to the juniors—giving them tips on taking the SAT." He tightens the imaginary tie again.

"Oh, yeah. Ian told me about it." Chris mimes a gagging gesture.

Zac sneers and walks away. Willa follows.

"Major douche," Chris says as we hurry to class.

"I know. I have no idea what she sees in him."

"Probably six to eight inches." Chris gestures the length with his hands.

"Oh my god, you whore." I slug him. "But you know something? I miss her—hanging with her."

"You miss the Willa that needed you."

"You're probably right. And she *so* doesn't need me anymore; that's for sure."

Chris wraps his arm around my shoulder. "You did a great thing for her."

"I just wish she didn't need a boyfriend to rely on."

"Well, she does. Not everyone's strong like my best buddy."

Mrs. Hogan, our art teacher, jumps up from her chair as we enter the room. "Bea, there you are!" She wears a few hats at the school. Not only is she the art teacher, she's also the counselor, nurse, librarian—and no, she doesn't wear the hats very well. Her eyes lit up once she found out that I was "an artist" (*oh my gosh, Bea, you can draw*), realizing that she could spend fifty minutes every Wednesday and Friday reading trashy novels or gossip mags, pretending that she had sick students to tend to or library books to check out (even though most kids don't read books here and certainly have never checked anything out of a library).

She hands me her thick paperback textbook. "I have to see a couple students in the office. They think they have mono."

"It's probably allergies," I say, blowing my nose.

"You think you could get the class started on the new-expressions chapter?"

"New expressions?" It sounds like a cheesy choral group. "Neo-expressionism, you mean?"

She looks at me, wide-eyed. "Sure. It's chapter four. Make up a project . . . like you did for the Cuban period. That was fun, very inspiring . . ." She waves, dismissing me, or rather dismissing herself, and is out the door.

"You mean Cubism . . . ," I say to no one.

A couple students grab their backpacks and make a beeline for the door. Nerdy Nate Menchel feverishly texts. Eva Marie twists her 'fro with some white goop from a tub as she chomps on a stick of gum to the beat of whatever she's listening to in her earphones.

Billy Weisman, perpetually high, yet unbelievably smart—he's seriously the übergenius of the senior class (and he looks like Shaggy from *Scooby-Doo*—even has a scraggly soul patch on his chin)—lopes on over to an open window with his low, baggy jeans, turns his Detroit Tigers baseball cap backward on his head, and lights up a cigarette. He squints at me and slings me some slang: "Yo, so prof Wash—what's innit fo' us, homey?"

I laugh. "Good question, Billy." I flip through the textbook—take a look at the neo-expressionism era: Basquiat's, Clemente's, and Schnabel's vivid, colorful paintings projecting raw, violent emotion that influenced artists like Andy Warhol. I chalk out the word *pop art* in three-dimensional bubble letters on the board.

"That's cool." Billy nods, approving. "Got yo' graffiti groove goin' on."

Nate raises his hand.

"Nate, you don't have to raise your hand. It's just me."

He clears his throat. "Graffiti art? That's pop art?"

"No, not exactly. But it definitely influenced street art."

Billy hoists his jeans, his cigarette dangling from his mouth, chalks out some graffiti scribble, touting his well-known tagging skills.

"Billy's the Banksy of Ann Arbor." Eva Marie pulls out her earphones.

"Dunno 'bout that anymore. Got the coppers hot on my tail—for taggin' shit."

"Seriously? You've been arrested?" I ask.

He nods. "Nabbed for train bombin'."

Hmmm . . . A tagger—maybe that would work. But I'd need a look. . . .

"Hey, Eva Marie. That thing you're doing with your hair." I eye her handiwork.

"Twisting?"

"Yeah. You think you could do it to me? Like, later today?" She blows a bubble, pops it. "Sure. I have a free after lunch. You?"

"PE, but I have no prob skipping it." In fact, I'm always looking for an excuse to dodge it. I'll probably have to run at least four marathons to graduate to make up for all the absences, but, what the heck. . . . I'll face that when I have to.

"Your hair'll be a cinch, Bea. It's not that tight on the curl scale, and I need the practice for cosmetology school. Meet me in the science hall john at one." She sticks her wad of gum up under the top of her desk, humming something while twisting the other side of her head.

I prop up the textbook on the chalkboard ledge, and while looking at Eva Marie, sketch out Andy Warhol's banana with yellow chalk.

"Sweet. That's the cover of the album *The Velvet Underground*," Eva Marie calls out. "I was just listening to Lou Reed."

"You were? Wow, I didn't know," I lie.

"Yeah, right," Chris mumbles under his breath.

Eva Marie switches her phone to speaker mode and turns up the volume on Lou Reed's "Walk on the Wild Side." She starts dancing, swinging her hips and swaying to the tune.

Nate joins in, awkwardly singing. She responds, pulling him from his chair, and placing her hands on his hips, singing, "Doo do doo do doo do do . . ."

Chris makes it a threesome, sandwiching an all-of-a-sudden extremely nervous Nate. The sax starts riffing. Billy stubs out his cigarette in a wilted potted plant on the sill, takes Eva Marie's arm, and twirls her around.

I'm chalking in the finishing touches on the banana when Mrs. Hogan comes barreling into the room. "What in heaven's name is going on in here?" She snatches Eva Marie's phone and silences the song.

Nate sits, clasps his hands.

"And what is that?" She points at the banana on the board.

Billy speaks up. "Prof Wash was getting us hip on pop art. Chap four. Like you said."

"That's ridiculous—that's not art."

"Actually, it is, and was heavily influenced by neo-expressionism. Bea taught us that," Nate explains.

She sniffs the air. "I smell smoke. Was someone having a cigarette . . . ? Billy! Do I have to send you down to the principal's office again?"

"Oh, no, it wasn't Billy, Mrs. Hogan." I jump in. "I saw someone outside smoking by the window. I smell it, too." I do a wavy thing in front of my nose, the chalk still in my hand. "Gross."

Mrs. Hogan holds her stomach. "Class is dismissed."

"But we still have another twenty minutes," Nate stupidly says.

She shoos us away and plops down in her chair. "Go study or something. Please go."

I quickly erase what I've drawn on the chalkboard.

Billy slings his backpack over his shoulder and whispers, "You're the bomb, Beawash." He then fist-bumps me and strolls out of the classroom.

"What a bitch Hogan is," Chris says.

"We have to cut her a break. I think she has a stomach problem, an ulcer or something."

"What?"

"Her belly is on fire, like, her insides were burning up when I was drawing at the chalkboard," I whisper.

"Unreal. You can do that thing with chalk, too?"

"Jesus, Chris. You make it sound like an STD or something."

"Well, sometimes I wish it *were* contagious. Then at least *I* could draw the truth out of Ian."

"Give it a rest, Chris. Ian really digs you—it's obvious. Come on, I need a smoke."

"I thought you were quitting."

"Cutting back. First one today."

We head toward the senior courtyard when Marsha

Wheaton, a fellow classmate, passes us crying, almost sobbing, running toward the lav.

Another guy rushes the hall, jumps, high-fiving, pumping the air with his fists. "Yessssss."

The school is suddenly buzzing—like an alarm went off.

"What's going on?" I ask.

"I don't know." Chris's phone dings. "Huh. It's an e-mail from . . . oh, shit . . . U of M. Bea, hold my hand. . . ."

I do, and he reads.

"Oh my god, oh my god, oh my god." Chris adds to the buzz, picks me up, and spins me around. "I got in, Bea! University of Michigan art department. Whoo-hoo!" he bellows, his arms splayed in the air.

"Well, duh, did you ever have any doubt?"

"This is friggin' awesome." He dances a little jig.

I stand back and take it in—observe him from a distance. Chris hugs Randall Pols—he's never hugged Randall Pols before; I didn't know he even knew him—but now that they just realize that they're both Wolverines, University of Michigan–bound, they bond.

I knew this day would happen—knew it would come. I'll never fit in in that way, the collegiate way—another one of the *shoulds*. Even if I wanted to, forced myself—it would make my parents so happy, especially my dad—it'd be phony, fake, not me. But Chris is different; this is the right move for him.

He looks my way, and I see his enthusiasm stall. I *so* don't want to be that person. I don't want to ruin it for him, be the

Eeyore in the room, so I muster up a killer smile and give him another big hug. Surprisingly, tears come to my eyes, and my throat catches a little. I suck it up. "I'm really happy for you, Chris."

He pulls back, peers into my eyes. "You okay?"

"Of course, you fool." I slap his shoulder.

His eyes snap back to wild, wide excitement. "Your dad's amazing."

"I'm sure my dad helped, being the art chair and all, but it was your awesome photography that got you in. Your portfolio is sick, dude."

Chris bounces on his toes as we join other nicotine fiends in the school courtyard.

"Did you know? Tell me. Did you? Were you hiding it from me?" He pants like a puppy dog.

"Had no idea. He didn't let on. But then again, he hasn't been home much—he's being considered for dean."

"This is so friggin' amazing, but you know the only thing that could top this? If you were going, too."

"Yeah, well, I'm not." I lean against a brick wall and feel it snag my sweater, and I light up.

"I still don't get it, Bea. It's a no-brainer for you. You've got the grades, the talent—"

"And the dad. I can't go to his school. It'd be too weird; you know that. I need to get out on my own, Chris. Out from under Mommy and Daddy. Maybe get my own apartment."

"Yeah, and what will Mommy and Daddy say about that?"

"What do you think?" I chew on a hangnail and crouch. "They're still all over me—need to know where I am all the time, what I'm doing, who I'm seeing. Sometimes I feel as if I can't breathe, like I'm being smothered."

Chris coughs at the dense smoke and sits down next to me. "I have an idea. . . . We could get an apartment together. That would be so awesome."

"Yeah, that would be super fun, wouldn't it?" He'll be in the dorm. He knows it, and knows that I know it. He's just being sensitive, and I love him for that. "Chris . . ."

"Yeah?"

"I've been thinking about something . . . um, haven't told anyone about it yet."

"What?"

"It's kind of a crazy idea, but . . ." I show him the tabbed section filled with inked designs in my sketchbook. "I'm thinking about getting my license as a tattoo artist."

"You're kidding me."

"I'm not."

He's about to check out my designs, when Nate Menchel bursts into the courtyard, howling like a wolf—very unlike Nate.

"U of M?" Chris asks him, handing me back my sketchbook.

Nate is speechless—madly nods, dumps out all his books from his backpack, and stomps on them. Chris jumps up and joins in the stomping. Like two little boys going to town, splashing in a mud puddle.

I walk away.

6 days
11 hours
30 minutes

With all the rushing around this morning, I totally spaced, forgot to pack a lunch, and Chris warned me to never buy food from the creepy googly-eyed lunch lady. And there seems to be a celebratory senior lunch fight going on in the cafeteria, because of the college acceptances, I guess. It looks as if Nate was doused with a carton of chocolate milk, a few cold cuts landed on top of Chris's head, and Principal Nathanson, trying to break up the festivities, slipped on a clump of mac and cheese. Fell flat on his ass.

Yeah . . . I think I'll bop on home and pick something up.

I turn the corner into my neighborhood and make my way through the woodsy, tree-canopied streets, open my window, and let the wind whip through my hair; then, of course, I sneeze at the sweet smell of budding jasmine. I'm about to pull into my driveway, when a white SUV shoots out in front of me and cuts me off.

"Hey, watch where you're going, buddy!" I yell out the window, but he's long gone down the road. I catch my breath and park.

It's been almost twelve years since we moved here. My dad had just been appointed chair of the art department at the University of Michigan, and it was a huge deal—a big move for us. I was six. It was midsummer—before the school year started up for my dad. I was about to enter first grade at the all-girl's school, Athena Day. We pulled our U-Haul truck up to what I thought was the most beautiful house I'd ever seen. A fairy-tale house. Magical, two stories, like my Barbie dollhouse. It had a big, green front lawn, surrounded by a split-rail wooden fence.

Mom dashed to the front door, jiggled the keys, and had to kick the bottom of the door till it opened. Dad stood in the driveway, his hands on his hips, smiling, watching her. "I'll fix that Bella—get to it right away. Won't be a problem."

And I made a beeline to the humongous tree that stood in the middle of the front yard. "Look at this, Dad."

"It's a sycamore, Bea."

I gazed up at its towering limbs and hugged it hard. My little arms reached halfway around its trunk. Having lived in the city of Chicago my whole life, I'd never seen, let alone touched, a tree this big. I kissed the bark; my nose smooshed against the mottled wood. It smelled like cold, wet dirt and stirred up something in my belly that made me feel, I don't know, home, grounded, safe.

I reached up and wrapped my legs around a heavy limb and then climbed the branches, scratching my bony knees.

"Be careful, Beatrice," Mom called out, laughing, as she stepped outside on the front stoop. I went as high as I could—before the branches spread too far apart. Then I sat back against the trunk, breathing hard, tucked and nestled in a comforting crook of the tree, and peered into a dormered window on the second floor of my new house.

It was framed with dark wood shutters that looked like they could close. (I found out later they were just ornamental, after I tried to shut them from the inside, almost fell out the window, and broke one shutter off its hinge.) A slanted ceiling with a wood beam split the room in half. "Oh, Daddy, I want that bedroom," I called out, pointing.

"You got it," he said. "It's yours."

I looked around my new neighborhood—saw a dog chasing a cat across the street, a man riding a lawn mower two houses over, some boys playing football in the next yard. I felt as if I were a fairy princess on top of the world, looking down on my kingdom.

How simple life seemed back then. How happy we were, the three of us—excited for the future. All the possibilities . . .

I sigh and walk toward the front door. The shutter on my bedroom window still dangles from the hinge; the paint is peeling. Dandelions poke through the weedy, unmowed lawn; one of the wooden rails of the fence lies on the ground, rotting. My dad is crazy busy with his job, and now wanting to be promoted to dean, he's rarely home and is too tired to work on the house on the weekends. And Mom? She bitches about it, but she'd rather spend her time painting children's murals on bedroom walls than painting the house. So the house looks lived-in, a little rough around the edges, but "perfectly fine with its imperfections," Dad says.

The front door still sticks. I give a little kick at the worn, splintered bottom—the same place it's been kicked at for the past twelve years. I start to walk toward the kitchen when I hear footsteps above. "Mom? Is that you? You home?"

She suddenly appears at the top of the stairs, looking flustered as she ties a robe around her slender waist. Her long, dark, gray-streaked curly hair is tousled; mascara is smeared under her long lashes.

"Jesus, Mom, you scared me."

"You scared me, too. What are you doing home?"

"Forgot my lunch."

She hurries down the stairs, into the kitchen. "You want me to make you something?"

"I thought you had a client meeting . . . the mural you're painting in Bloomfield Hills?"

"No. No. The dad cancelled. I guess I slept in a little." She sweeps her hair back behind her ears and adjusts her robe.

I sneeze. "Ugh. My allergies are horrible, and my nose won't stop running. Can you please get me a Claritin?"

"Sure, hon." She pulls out a chair, stands on it, and unlocks a combination padlock on a kitchen cabinet over the refrigerator.

"You don't have to hide stuff anymore, Mom, you know that, right?"

She doesn't answer, just pulls out a foil sheet of the allergy medicine, pops out a tablet, and hands me the pill.

My parents insist on locking up stuff ever since my over-dose: everything from the bottle of scotch that my dad likes to sip now and then, to vanilla extract (as if I'd consider getting drunk on two ounces of a decade-old bottle of flavoring). And the Claritin. I mean, what am I going to do with allergy medi-cine? Snort it? Oh. Yeah, I think I did try that once.

It's sad that they don't trust me yet. But I made that bed, for sure. It's like I'm their handicapped child and want, need to kick the crutches out from underneath me.

I lower my head under the faucet, slurp up water, and swallow the pill. "Oh, by the way, I'm going to hit a meeting after school, so I probably won't be home till dinner." I have to cover my butt, not knowing how long Sergeant Daniels will need me.

"Says here you already went to one before school." She stands at the counter reading the note I'd left.

Shit. "Oh, yeah, well, I got sidetracked with Willa and ended up not going. Something about a birthday party for me." *Not a total lie.*

"Well, that's sweet of her." She pours herself a cup of cold coffee—heats it in the microwave. "Then I'll see you at dinner. Takeout, okay?"

"Sure, I'm fine with whatever." I kiss her on the cheek and smell something different—a musky, smoky smell.

Her phone buzzes in the pocket of her robe. She reads the message and smiles.

"Who's that?"

"Oh, no one. Something about work," she says as she rushes back up the stairs, forgetting about her coffee, texting the *no one* back. "Have a good day, hon."

"Sure." *What the hell was that about?*

6 days
10 hours
15 minutes

I sit on the bleachers at the top of the Packard High stadium,
watching my PE class run relays on the track below. Eva
Marie was right. My hair was a cinch to twist and didn't take
her long. I could join in on the relays or open my Moleskine
and sketch out possible "tagger looks." Duh, easy decision.

"Cool 'do." Billy Weisman checks out my hair and smiles as
he balances on his skateboard, teetering on the steps. I guess
he's cutting class, too.

I pat at the pinned twists. "Thanks. Eva Marie did an
awesome job."

"Hey, thanks for covering for me with Hogan—the smoke
thing."

"No prob."

He bends his knees, stretches out his arms, leans his body
forward, and begins to surf down the stairs, zigzagging, jumping
gracefully from one row to another, zipping like a razor. His

movements are effortless, fluid. He approaches the steel railing above the football field, leaps up, and his feet land, balanced, crouched on the rail. He tucks his head close to his chest and ends the performance with a tight forward somersault in the air, nailing the landing with both feet on the ground, arms raised like a gymnast.

I applaud and give him a mental ten. Billy hitches up his baggy pants, vaults the railing, and jogs back up the bleacher steps, not even close to being out of breath, even though he's a big-time smoker . . . of many substances.

"That was amazing, Billy. Is there anything you can't do?"

Billy walks out of the stadium and over to a pop machine standing against the school wall, kicks it, gets us two free bottles of Coke, and hands me the soda as we sit on top of a chained-down picnic table. He lights up a joint and talks while inhaling, sounding like a muffled sock puppet. "Shit. You're clean, right?" He hides it behind his back.

"Yeah. Just blow the other way."

He does, exhaling a pretty line of silver smoke. He peers at me sideways. "Really, no prob?"

I shrug. I'm not sure what it's like for Billy. I have no idea what his story is, but, yeah, it's a problem for me. Every day. And yet, oddly, it also exhilarates me, the challenge of it all when the craving, the urge sticks out its big ugly face, like, *What are you going to do, fool?* Singsonging, *I'm stronger than you are, neener neener neener.*

So this is what I do: I carry around bright-red boxing

gloves—in my head. And every time those words, the urge, that monster appears—even dares to—I do a one-two punch: uppercut to the jaw and then a left to the cheek. (I perfected it, for real, with the creep that raped Willa last fall.) Then I imagine the craving as a fizzle of impotent excrement dripping down to the ground, burying itself in a hole in the earth in shame, I kick dirt over it, stomp on it, and move on . . . until the next time—which could easily be five minutes later.

I also know that using again would shackle me, take me down into that hole. I *would* be handicapped. And do I really want to live with my parents, or be thrown back into rehab—or worse, on the streets—for the rest of my life? Live the life of a loser chump?

Billy stubs out the joint. "What's poppin', home skillet?"

I laugh. "I love the way you talk, your *speak*. . . . It's so cool."

"Da gangsta Billy rap?"

"You're in a gang?"

"I gotta taggin' crew goin' on. But gang? Shit, no. I'm just innit for my art." He raises his arms and slings off some hand gestures.

"Whoa. Let me see that tat on your arm."

He smiles, lifts the sleeve of his T-shirt, exposing a detailed tattoo of the brain—the swirls of the four lobes wrapped around his upper arm.

"That's amazing. Where'd you get inked?"

"I have this bro. Stan the Man. He has his own tat shop down on Main."

"Huh." I take out a cigarette—ready to light. "Um, you know . . . I've been thinking about getting into tatting."

"Get out. That's stupendous." He slaps the table. "You got some of your art on you?"

I put the cigarette back in the pack. "Seriously? You want to see my designs?"

"Fuck, yeah."

"Well, I've never really shared them with anyone. . . . It's probably just a stupid dream."

"Stupid? Bullshit. A dream starts here." He points to the right side of his brain tat. "Come on, hand it over, lemme see."

He leafs through the pages of my sketchbook, intently studying, outlining them gently with his finger as if they're alive, three-dimensional. *He's so high.*

I lace up the imaginary boxing gloves—again—swallow the last slug of pop, and toss the bottle in the overflowing recycling bin next to the chained-down trash can.

"I've always known you could draw, but damn, this is inspired," Billy murmurs.

"Yeah, you think so?"

"Is the Weisman wise? I'd let you ink me in a sec. And Stan . . . the man could teach you the ropes."

"Oh my god, that would be so incredible."

A car screeches out of the parking lot, music blaring through the stereo. A screaming senior hangs out the window: "Screw you, Packard High!"

I look at Billy. "Guess he got into college."

"Or not." Billy laughs. "So, what does your dad think about you inkin'? Isn't he like a VIP dude at Michigan?"

"He doesn't know."

"Hah, ditchin' a BFA for a TAT."

"Yeah, the whole situation stinks. He thinks I'm going to defer for a year, expects me to live at home—and my mom, she wants me to work with her, painting murals for kids' bedrooms. Her business has picked up."

Billy snorts. "You? Painting puppy dogs and kitty cats? No effin way."

"I know, right? What about you, Billy? What are your plans after graduation?"

"Gonna help my pop out at the tire shop. Fitting semis. He deals and wheels 'em." His eyes are red and squinty as he strokes his goatee. "So, you wanna go train-bombin' with me? See my shit?"

"I thought you said the cops were after you."

"That's the fun." He flings some more gang-speak. "Throw up some tags, slide and hide, and ditch the bacon."

My phone buzzes with a text from Daniels—*the bacon*:

DANIELS: c u at 4. Don't be late.

"Hey, Billy . . . you mind if I borrow your hat? I'll get it back to you tomorrow."

He pulls the cap off his head, slaps it on mine. "Fo' sho'. You did me a solid, Beawash. It's yours to keep."

"And you think you could teach me some of da Billy rap?"

6 days
7 hours
55 minutes

My hands are cuffed behind my back. Sergeant Daniels, now in his uniform blues, with the three gold stripes on his sleeve, pulls me through the busy Ann Arbor Police Station. My baggy "fat" jeans from the backseat of my car slide down on my butt, my high-top Converse sneakers squeak as I trip on the linoleum-tiled floor. "Slow down, shit!" I cry out, acting like I'm out of breath.

The Sarge glances at me, his eyes squint with confusion, and I give him a little smile—for a nanosecond—and then slap the mask of phony urgency back on my face as that jerk, Detective Cole, passes us. I huff and grunt, pretend that the sergeant is yanking and twisting my arm. Cole smirks and nods at Daniels. *He doesn't recognize me . . . yessss.* I'm just another low-life punk that got caught doing something bad—another one down.

The sergeant joins in on the charade and orders, "Get in there. Now."

I fake a snivel as he shoves me into a stuffy room, slams the door shut, and locks it.

We both sigh. The performance is over—curtain closed.

"Jesus, Bea. What was that all about?"

"I wanted it to look real, not like you dragged me in here for friggin' jaywalking or something. I had to play a part, come on." I struggle with the cuffs on my wrists. "Hey, can you help me with these things? I kind of need my hands to work."

"Sure." He closes in on me—reaching around my back and unlocking the handcuffs—pauses for a beat. Our bodies touch slightly, our breath in sync. The woodsy smell socks me in the stomach . . . again.

Sergeant Daniels backs away, hooking the cuffs onto his belt, and I massage my sore wrists.

"I put them on really loose, Bea. If you hadn't struggled like that, they wouldn't have hurt."

"Yeah, well, you live and learn. That was the first time I've been cuffed, thank god—and hopefully the last." I pull the sleeves down on Chris's oversize red hoodie sweatshirt and yank the jeans up over the elastic on a pair of men's striped boxers (I wear them sometimes over black tights, on casual days).

The sergeant checks me out. "What the hell are you wearing?"

I wag my finger at him. "Don't you mad dawg me."

"What? What did you say?"

"I said, don't look at me that way—up and down, all

judgy-like. The case is gang-related, so I wanted to look the part. Got my taggin' duds on."

"I said the *case* is gang-related, not you."

I yank Billy's oversize Detroit Tigers baseball cap off my head.

"And what did you do to your hair?"

"My GF twisted then pinned it. What's your beef?"

"You look like a boy."

I place the cap backward on my head, scrunch my shoulders forward, slouch, and sign out the word *cop* with my hands—like Billy showed me. "Yeah, well, you look like bacon, a pig, in those duds."

"Now what are you doing?"

"I'm throwing you signals—stacking—slinging some hand signs, dude. I did a little gangsta research after we convened."

Daniels shakes his head, laughs. "You don't do anything half-assed, Bea, that's for sure." He gestures for me to sit in a chair in front of a desk. A large window looks down on a cinder-block room. A young black kid sits alone on a folding chair behind a table. He looks scared—petrified, like he's about to pee his baggy jeans. Tats peek out on his neck from beneath his sweatshirt.

"That's him?"

"Yeah. Junior."

"Damn. He's a BG."

"A what?"

"Baby gangster. You sure he's seventeen?"

Junior checks out the room—his eyes wide with fear—and then stops. Focuses on me, his gaze burrowing through me.

I jump. "Whoa. Can he see me?"

"No. It's a one-way mirror. But he probably knows someone's observing him."

His baby-sweet face with wide-set, dark eyes drips with innocence. His full lips turn down and quiver, like he's fighting back tears. "You're right. He didn't do it."

The sergeant leans in. "Wait. Are you seeing something already? What he's thinking?"

"No, of course not. I'm not drawing." I scoff.

"Oh. Okay. Right."

"He just looks so sweet."

"You need paper? A pen?"

"How long have you known me?" I pull my Moleskine and a pen out of a Pokémon backpack. I passed a yard sale on the way over and bought it for a quarter—thought it went well with the "look"—and transferred all the shit from my purse into the backpack.

"I'm going in there—going to ask him a few questions— pretend he didn't confess to anything. I need to get him to talk. He knows something that he doesn't want to say; in particular, who planted the weed, who set him up, who killed the kid in the Huron. He's covering for someone."

"You need the 411 on the OG."

"The what?"

"Information on the original gangster. The boss in charge of it all—the big guns. Jesus, Daniels, you gotta get hip with the homeys." I sling a few nonsense signs.

The sergeant ignores my gang-speak.

"By the way, Sarge? He's not gonna rat someone out."

"I know all about the snitch rule, Bea."

"And just by looking at him? He's scared shitless about something."

"That's why I need you to draw. You ready?"

I crack my knuckles. "I'm ready."

"You got your phone with you?"

"Duh." I take it out of a backpack pocket, place it on the table.

"Text me when you get a hit on something, okay?"

"Okay." I put my pen to the page.

"And you'll let me know if anything makes you uncomfortable?"

"What are you talking about?"

"The drug part of this case. It hasn't been that long. That's all."

"Believe me, I know. You don't have to remind me." And then, looking into his eyes, a mukluk boot suddenly kicks me in the head—the boots I was wearing that night. It's what he's thinking about. My stomach sinks. "Sarge. I'm cool. Really, I am. You don't have to worry."

But the thought of it sucker punches me in the gut, and I know it does the same to Daniels as I watch him slouch at the memory and leave the room.

Damn. I hate thinking about it. It was so STUPID of me.

• • •

Last November I had just celebrated four months of sobriety and was so proud—until I saw him, my ex-boyfriend, and my ex–drug dealer, Marcus, waiting in his car as I scraped the ice off my windshield in the St. Anne's parking lot.

My first mistake was crossing the snowy street to his idling Prius.

"What the hell do you want, Marcus? Why are you here?" I asked.

"For you." He smiled his slippery smile. "I like your hair. It's sexy."

Pang #1.

"I told you to stay away from me."

"I told you I love you."

Pang #2.

"No, you didn't, Marcus. You never said you loved me."

"Well, I meant to."

"Yeah, right." I headed back to my car.

"I'm clean, Bea," he called out to me. "A week now. Nothing. Nada."

Pang #3.

I paused for a second and thought, *Could he be? Really?* Then I waved my hand, dismissing him. "Bullshit. It isn't that easy. I would know." And kept walking.

"It is if you want something . . . bad," he called out. "Like you."

Pang #4.

I reached my car and continued scraping the windshield. Maybe a little too hard. Chunks of ice flew off; some hit my face and immediately melted on my warm, flushed cheeks. A slow boil simmered in my belly—always had with his presence, and dammit, still did. I didn't know if it was him, us—the trippy, pheromonal phenomenon that crackled like electricity between our two bodies, or because of the drugs that he'd provided the last couple years. Probably both. I was addicted to both.

I heard his car door shut. His footsteps neared and squeaked on the packed snow. Behind me, Marcus wrapped his arms around my waist.

Pang #5.

"I just want to talk. I miss you, Bea," he whispered in my ear. Nuzzled his face in my neck.

No. Don't let him take you in.

I stuffed my freezing hands into my coat pocket. "I've worked hard for this night . . . these four months. You're not going to screw it up. Do you hear me?" I turned and yelled. But I knew it was too late; the ice was cracking under my feet.

I saw myself caving in the reflection of his round, wire-rim glasses. He took my hands out of my pocket; blew on them with his warm, moist breath; and lowered them to his chest, his heart. "Bea, I told you, I'm clean. I'm not using. I love you. I miss you so much."

Pang #6.

TKO.

I fell headfirst into those piercing, dark, hypnotic eyes— believed every word he uttered. Believed that he wanted, needed, desired me, like no one else ever had, and I disregarded the four months of sobriety I'd trudged through; said *screw you* to the months, the days, the hours, and to everyone who loved and cared about me. Chucked it, like a measly, melting ice chip into a snowdrift, only to be shoveled away by the approaching snowplow.

We ended up in Marcus's hobbit-like room at the top of a frat house on the University of Michigan campus. He majored in pharmaceutical medicine, and was, aptly, a campus drug dealer.

I woke up, lying in his bed. Glimpsed at the clock: two a.m.

Oh no, no, no, no, no. What have I done?

Whistler, his Maine coon cat, was curled up on my feet. He yawned, stretched, circled, and settled himself on Marcus's legs. I sat up, and the room started to spin, so I put one foot down on the cold wooden floor, grounding me. Marcus was asleep— mouth open, drool dripping. Stale, boozy-smelling snores. A bong sat on the side table. A half-empty bottle of tequila was lying on Marcus's naked belly, moving in sync with his breath.

The spinning stopped, but my brain felt heavy, thick with substance—as if it were coated with itchy alpaca wool that I couldn't get at and scratch.

I pulled the covers off my naked body and stood. Marcus groaned, rolled over, and faced the wall, away from me.

A window in his room was cracked open, and a gust of cold November air swept through, rustling the blinds. I started to shiver, and my stomach churned, sending a wave of nausea up through my body. My knees buckled. I was wasted. I stumbled to the john. Hung my head over the toilet and puked up tequila. It pooled in the toilet, spilled down the sides, splattered on my new mukluk boots which I'd kicked off earlier on the black-and-white tiled floor.

I hurled until my stomach was empty—but the smell made me dry heave—it felt like a hand had reached down my throat and yanked, tearing away at my intestines, bringing up my soul . . . whatever was left of it.

And then—a loud knock on the door. Sergeant Daniels's voice. "Bea. Are you in there? Bea. Answer me!"

Shit. I grabbed a towel hanging from a rack and wrapped it around myself.

Marcus stirred.

Another loud knock. "Open up, or I'll kick this door in!"

Marcus jumped up. "Fuck." He leaned over the bed, tried to grab his jeans—but not in time, as the sergeant did what he promised and barreled into the room.

Whistler hissed, ran under the bed.

I was leaning against the bathroom doorframe, the towel barely covering me. Marcus stood naked next to the bed.

Sergeant Daniels scanned the room. Looked at me, looked at Marcus. I thought I heard a throaty, growling noise—I wasn't sure if it was coming from Daniels or the cat.

Marcus grabbed a pillow and placed it over his limp dick and crouched, anticipating what came next.

I held out my hand. "Dan, don't . . ." But my words went unnoticed—flew out the window.

A good four inches taller, the sergeant placed his large, leather-gloved hands on Marcus's skinny shoulders, lifted him, and with teeth clenched, threw him against the wall.

Marcus crumbled to the ground and groaned, rolling into a fetal position.

"Stop it, Dan!" I screamed, but I was immediately silenced by the sergeant's raised hand.

"Stay away, Bea," he ordered.

Using the toe of his boot, he gently nudged Marcus, rolled him toward the bed, snatched a blanket, and tossed it on top of him. He then knelt down, flashed his police badge in Marcus's face, and seethed, spat, "You're going to leave today. Pack up all your shit, all of it, and you're going to get the hell out of Ann Arbor. Never come back—not ever to my city. And if you do, and believe me, I'll know if you do, I'll get a warrant and have your sorry, wimpy ass busted—locked away for good, for the rest of your miserable life. Do you hear me?"

Marcus coughed, moaned, and nodded.

Daniels stood. "Bea, get dressed."

I dropped the towel, quickly threw on my clothes, and crossed to the splintered door. I took one last look at the broken mess of Marcus on the floor and left the devil's den.

The sergeant drove. Made no eye contact with me.

My head pounded. "How did you find me? How'd you know where I was?"

His nostrils flared, steaming up the windows. "Spotted your car alone at St. Anne's. A snowplow was circling the lot. He said he saw a girl leave with someone in a Prius."

"How did you know it was Marcus?"

"That punk has been on campus police radar for a while. Wasn't hard to figure out."

"So you were following me again?" I shivered.

"I wanted to know if you could check out a perp for me— draw something out of him."

"You mean a case?"

"Yeah. But never mind."

"I'm sorry."

I eyed the sergeant—his profile, his jaw set in a determined clench. I willed him to look at me. But he didn't. He wouldn't face me. "It'll never happen again, I promise." I dropped my heavy head in my hands. "I'm sorry. So, so sorry."

"Yeah. I am, too."

Oh my god. They're going to send me back to rehab. I panicked. "Please don't tell my parents, please. They think I'm with

Willa." I grabbed on to the sleeve of his nubuck jacket. "I don't want to go back to rehab. I can't go back to that place. *Please.*"

He turned into a subdivision, past rows of modest ranch houses—every one, just like the last—pulled into a driveway, and stopped the engine.

Sergeant Daniels spoke as if he were talking to himself, convincing himself. "You're going to spend the rest of the night at my house. Max is with his mother, so you can sleep in his room. I'll take you to your car in the morning, and you'll drive straight home. Yes, I will follow you. And you'll do a thirty/thirty. Thirty AA meetings in thirty days—no exception—starting tomorrow. You agree to that and I won't tell your parents."

I blubbered with gratitude—snot ran down my face. "Oh, thank you. Thank you . . ."

"Okay. Let's get in the house. Take your boots off first. They smell like vomit."

I did—I stepped out of the mukluks, and holding my arm, he walked me into his dark house, brought me to his son, Max's, room. I sat on the bed. He took off my coat, gave me four saltine crackers, a glass of water, and two aspirins, and placed a puke bucket near the bed—*just in case*, he said.

The sergeant lifted a Spider-Man quilt, tucked me under it, and made eye contact for the first time. His sad green eyes bore through me, etched my brain.

"This is just a blip, Bea. Just a blip on the screen. It's not going to happen again, and no one needs to know about it. It will be our little secret." Then he kissed my forehead and left the room.

That night I dreamed of *my* superhero, Dan Daniels.

The next morning I found my boots sitting on the floor by the bed—clean. And I started one day, one hour, one minute . . . all over again.

• • •

I take a deep breath, unzip my sweatshirt, shake out my hands, and watch Sergeant Daniels enter the room, pull up a metal chair, and sit across the table from the kid, his back to me.

"So, Junior . . . may I call you that?" I hear his voice through the speakers imbedded in the wall.

Junior shrugs. His head hangs low—he doesn't make eye contact with the sergeant. His right knee rapidly jiggles up and down underneath the table.

"This doesn't have to be difficult—prolonged. Just give me the 411 on your OG. Who set you up?"

Hah. Quick study, Daniels, I think to myself.

Junior's voice cracks, straddles high and low. "I already told the other cop. I fessed up—it's all there." He points at a manila folder. "I called the shots—nobody else. There's nothin' more." His jaw sets in a grimace, and he shoots a well-rehearsed tough-guy look at the sergeant—but it doesn't fly. The look falls flat.

"Okay, whatever you say." Daniels leans back in his chair and reads from the folder.

I chew the tip of my pen, waiting for something to pop up. Junior's left leg joins in on the dance with his right, both legs jiggling so high they graze the underside of the table.

Daniels gets up from his chair and starts circling Junior. "You know what you're looking at, right? You're not considered a minor here in Michigan. They'll throw you in the big house, and I'm not talking about U of M's football stadium, we're talking *years*—maybe life. You're a good kid. No priors—squeaky clean record. I can throw that folder away—your confession—in the trash, right now, you know that, don't you?"

Junior chews the side of his mouth. His nostrils flare in silence.

"Are you taking a dive for someone? Maybe a bro? A homey? Someone close to you?" Junior's legs suddenly stop shaking.

Daniels glances up at me and then leans in close to Junior, and whispers, "So that's it. You're protecting someone you care about."

"I dunno know what you talkin' 'bout." Junior folds his arms in front of his chest and eyes the stained ceiling tiles as if he's trying to stop gravity from pulling down the tears.

Daniels walks around the table and sits. "You're young; you're smart. You have your whole life ahead of you."

Junior squints a pained look at Daniels.

And I squint at Junior. Trying to force something in my head. But it's empty—nothing is coming into focus. I drag my chair closer to the scratched glass, breathe on it, and wipe it with the sleeve of my hoodie and gaze into his eyes.

"Fine." Daniels doesn't let up. "You're guilty. Got it. With that confession?" He points at the folder. "You're basically toast—so why not? Why not tell me more?" He stands—sits on the table. "Why the hell would you kill a homey and dump him in the river? You got more going on, don't cha, Junior? What else you dealing? Where's the rest of the stash? There has to be more, a shitload more."

Junior looks right at me. I wait for something to kick in . . . what he's seeing—what he's thinking about. And his sad, scared eyes—his pupils start dancing around like he's suddenly focusing on something, reliving something. And in an instant a series of images start bouncing in my head, too, like a pinball machine. Balls. Dozens of lime-green, fuzzy tennis balls whirl around, slam against one another. My brain pulsates with each bounce. I try to keep my hand steady as I pencil them on the paper and then text Daniels:

ME: got it.

The sergeant reacts to the buzz of the phone in his back pocket. He takes it out and reads. "Excuse me one minute, will you? And while I'm gone? Think about everything I said. Think about your future. A cap and gown in June, or the slammer at seventeen." He exits the room.

Junior stays seated, blinks a few times, his gaze burrowing into me, as if he sees me through the mirror again—focused in tight, a lone tear wells up and then drips down on his cheek. He doesn't bother to wipe it away.

I jump as the sergeant charges in the room. "Why did that take you so long?"

"Sorry, jeez. I didn't know I was under the gun. Bad pun, I know."

"So? What did you see, draw?"

I tear out the page in my book, stand, hand it to him.

"What's this?"

"Looks like tennis balls to me."

He flips it around, checks out the back. "Where's the face?"

"What face?"

"The face you saw when you studied him?"

"I didn't see a face. I saw balls. Tennis balls."

"You were supposed to draw a face—the boss—the OG."

"I don't always see faces; you know that. Sorry. Fire me, why don't you? I draw what's in their mind." I shrug, sit back down on the chair. "Don't blame me; blame Junior. Damn, my head is hurting."

"Well, what the hell am I supposed to do with this?"

"I don't know. I have to figure that out for you, too?" I lean my elbows on my knees, lower my head, and rub my temples.

He studies the drawing—bites his bottom lip. "I'll give it to Cole. See what he can get out of this . . . maybe send the canines in there."

"Not Cole—he'll screw it up."

"Bea, don't tell me how to do my job."

"I'm not. It's just that Junior's scared about something, Sarge. His eyes were, like, crazy scared."

The sergeant doesn't respond for a moment. "Well, I need more than this. I've got to get more out of him somehow."

I feel like such a failure. "What happens to him now?"

"We'll keep him in the holding cell for the time being."

"The holding cell? Where's that?"

"In the basement."

I stand. "Put me in there with him. I can get more out of him, without glass between us, and maybe draw something that'll help."

"Don't be crazy. That's too dangerous. And you're a girl. You wouldn't be allowed in there with him."

"You said I look like a guy."

"No way, Bea. No."

"Come on. . . . I'm sure there are cameras, right? You can watch. I'll be fine."

"I don't know about this. . . ."

"I do. I can draw the truth out of him. I know I can. Give me another chance. Please?"

• • •

We have to play the game again—but this time we switch roles: it's the sergeant who's acting tough for an approaching deputy as he shoves me down the fluorescent-lit basement hallway. "I've got her . . . I mean him," Daniels explains. "And believe me, you don't want to handle him. He's a biter."

A biter? Really, I'm a biter? I eye him like he's crazy.

The sergeant gives me a hint of a smile and then pushes me into a small jail cell and unlocks the handcuffs—nope, not the last time I had to wear them. He gestures with his head toward a security camera, leans in close, and whispers, "Stand right where you are and turn your cap around on your head when you've got something. That'll be our signal. But make sure I see you do it. I'll be right around the corner, monitoring, and I'll get to you within a minute. You got it, Bea?"

"Got it, Sarge."

He slams the steel bars shut. They *clang*—lock automatically.

I look around at the cell. Probably six by eight feet. I pace the space and prove my estimation right. It smells of pissy Pine-Sol. Three sterile cinder-block walls painted a drab olive green; a concrete floor; a stainless toilet and sink jutting out of the wall; a worn wooden plank to sit on, lie on, wait on, worry on. Phony amenities, bullshit hope.

Black scuff marks mar the floor; the words *fuck you all*, scraped by someone, probably with a fingernail, are etched in the wood on the side of the plank. The metal bars are worn, the finish dulled from clenched fists.

This could have so been my life. Spent in a cell. Locked away. I was never busted—never had to sit in a hole like this.

It was bad enough overdosing—waking up in a hospital, being thrown into rehab by my parents. But here? It's stupid scary. That's what it's meant to do, this place. Shame you. Entrap you. Mess with your head.

My stomach tightens. I get cold and hot at the same time, and I suddenly start to sweat. My heart does a fluttery thing, like a fish tail flopping back and forth, desperate to free itself from the bottom of a boat. I sit down on the bench, try to breathe deeply, slowly—but it's not working. I wipe my upper lip with my sleeve. My throat feels as if it's closing up. *Holy crap. I'm having a panic attack. I've got to get out of here. Daniels . . . I need him.*

I'm about to look in the camera and turn my hat around when I suddenly hear keys jingling. But not the sergeant's keys. It's the deputy escorting Junior—leading him into the cell across from me. Junior complies, his big feet dragging along behind. The bars clang shut, and the now familiar "locked-in-my-brain-for-the-rest-of-my-life" echo bounces off the drab green walls.

Junior pays no attention—doesn't even notice me. He starts to circle like a crazed animal, banging, hitting the bars. And my heart slows, my breath softens. . . . And I climb up, taking me out of myself—out of the hole. It's about him now—not me.

"What you in for?" I ask, sounding like a stupid line from a TV cop show.

He ignores me, still circling.

I try again. "What's crackin', homey?"

He snarls, "I ain't your homey."

Junior walks to the back of the cell—places his hands up above his head, leaning them on the cinder blocks, his legs splayed like he's about to be frisked, and proceeds to hit his forehead over and over against the wall, repeating the words *shit, shit, shit.*

"Dude, chill out, you're going to bust your head open. And I'm not cool with blood."

He stops for a beat and yells, "Shut the fuck up!"

"I'm just tryin' to make conversation."

"I said, shut the fuck up."

I have to get him to stop, sit, still himself, and face me. I have to reach him somehow, read his eyes. *Think, Bea.*

"Can I tell you a secret?" I talk through the bars.

Junior ignores me and continues his slamming. "Hey," I whisper, hoping the sergeant can't read lips. "I'm a chick, pretending to be a guy. Wanna see?"

I figure this will get his attention. And I'm right; it does. He stops his banging, whips around, like, *what the hell?*

"Check it out."

Junior rubs the red welt on his forehead with his palm and slowly makes his way to me, looks in both directions down the corridor, probably making sure no one's watching, ready to take on the pending peep show.

I've never been into this before, exposing myself, sexting— but whatever it takes. I step back so the sergeant doesn't see me in the camera, and slowly unzip my jacket, exposing my wrinkled PE tee, size small, and shrunk in the wash. Even though I'm not exactly well-endowed, no way does it hide the girls.

Junior sits on the wooden bench, his eyes focused on me—I don't think he even blinks—and his leg starts jiggling again. But this time it appears to be a "seventeen-year-old-trying-not-to-get-a-boner-from-a-tight-T-shirt jiggle."

"What the hell you doin' here? You nuts?" His jaw juts back and forth.

"Shhh. They don't know. I told them I lost my license." I zip up. "I wouldn't be here in the guys' cell if they knew, and I sure don't wanna be thrown in with them mean bitches. Girls are badder than boys, you know that, right? They scratch and shit."

I get him to smile a little. "Oh, man, that's for sure. The bitches in my 'hood, they're . . ." He stops. Cracks his neck.

"Where's your 'hood?"

He drops his eyes. Says nothing.

"You won't tell nobody about my boobs, right?" I whisper.

His eyes zero in on me. "I ain't no rat. Never will be," he hisses.

"That's cool." I sit and try to keep the conversation chill. "Did I really fool ya? You thought I was a guy? It's crazy wild I'm getting away with it."

He wrinkles his brow and shrugs his shoulders. "I don't know how you fooled them, but I didn't get a good look at you. I woulda known, though, if I did." He chews on his thumb, nods, still studying me like I'm a figment of his imagination. "So what d'you do, anyway; why you here?" He spits a piece of nail out on the floor.

The "tagging bust scenario" feels too lame for this sitch, so I say, "I was picked up for lifting an effin laptop at the mall and got caught, and I was carrying dope in my pack. Can you believe it?" I finger the worn wood of the bench. "Stupid, right?"

"Shit, yeah."

I keep going, bolstering the charade. "Only way I can make money lately? Lifting and then selling." I pull out a little spiral pad of paper and a pen that the sergeant stuffed in my back pocket. "Okay, I told you my deal, now it's your turn. What you in for?"

He sucks through his teeth as if he's swallowing a spit secret and lies down on his back on his bench. He stares at the ceiling.

I start doodling.

He glances over, sits up a bit, leaning on an elbow. "How come you got a pen? They don't let that shit in here."

"I know; I smuggled it in—shoved it up my ass." I hold it out toward him. "Wanna borrow it?"

He smiles again, and I think I hear a little laugh—short-lived.

I look around the cell, falsely befriending it. "You know, this is the best place I've been in the last week. It has a toilet, a sink—both stainless—top of the line, like a four-star hotel."

A definite snicker. "You wandering?" He sniffs.

"Kinda," I say. "I got in a big fight with the 'rents, and they kicked me out. You know . . . tough love, they say. More like tough shit, I say. So, yeah, I'm on the run, chillin', trying to stay out of trouble." I laugh. "I guess I messed up that last part."

"You on the streets?"

I nod. "But the bathrooms in the malls are cool for whore baths. You know, chick parts."

He looks away, kind of shifts his body over to the other side. *I went too far, dammit. Gotta get him back.* "TMI? Sorry, man, I didn't mean to share that. I'm doing the best I can, dodging the pigs. And it's a lot easier pretending I'm a guy. I don't get messed with, if you know what I mean."

He leans forward, wraps his arm around his knees. "Oh, yeah, you gotta get off the streets. You don't wanna get hurt. It's nasty out there. I know a couple chicks that've been hit hard. Sliced."

"Sliced?"

"Yeah, even by other girls. They go for your face. Don't want you to be too pretty. And the dudes wanna claim you. It's good you dress like that."

Unbelievable. All the heat he's dealing with, and he's worried about me? Giving me advice? Wow. He's so not guilty—no way. "Yeah, I gotta do what I gotta do—acting tough, dressin' butch. But if I'm honest? I'm scared out of my mind."

He doesn't have to utter a word, but he's scared, too—his chin rests on top of his knees tightly tucked, hugging his body.

I draw his face on the pad. The beardless jaw, broad nose,

the jagged scar etched in his skin above his upper lip. His hair is closely cropped, forming a perfectly straight line stretching across his high forehead, and his eyes are round like big, wet black buttons.

Junior releases his knees and stretches his long legs out on the bench. "What you drawing?"

"You." I tear the page off, crumble up the piece of paper, and throw it to him under the bars—under the camera, I hope.

He sits up, bends over, grabs it, and folds the paper flat. "Damn. That looks like me. You an artist or something?"

"Or something. I do tats, a little taggin', train bombin'."

"I probably cleaned up your art."

"Huh?"

"Forget it." He looks away. "I said too much."

"Well, what else we gonna do to pass the time? We might as well shoot the shit." I think about the tennis balls, wondering what they mean. "You into sports?"

"Sure. Why you ask that?"

"I dunno. You look buff, is all. Not that I'm checking you out or nothin'." I smile at him.

He smiles back. "I do a little running, lift weights and stuff with a team."

"Oh, yeah, where?"

"Around."

And it happens again . . . crackling fire this time, burning its way into my head like a branding iron: the image—slowly, menacingly, ferociously—takes a swat at and grabs a hold of my mind's eye. A bear claw flashes in front of me, through me, travels down my right hand, and I draw the claw on the page. I scratch out the furry paw on the paper in front of me—unsheathed, threatening sharp talons. And my head feels as if it's been torn open.

Two images in one day—and I'm paying for it big time. The room starts to spin. I lower my head between my knees, and the pad of paper falls to the floor.

Junior jumps up off the bench. "What the hell is that?" He backs up against the rear wall of his cell.

"A claw?" I eke out.

"Who the fuck *are* you? Why did you draw that?"

I squeeze the back of my neck. I'm in too much pain to lie. "I dunno. 'Cause you were thinking of one. That's how it normally happens."

"What you talking about?"

It feels like a nail is lodged, stuck in my brain. "It's crazy, I know, but I see stuff. Sometimes stuff I don't want to see—what other people are thinking, but only when I draw." I approach the bars, my vision blurred now.

"Get the hell away from me, you freak." He hugs the back wall.

The room keeps spinning, and I fight to stand on my two feet. "You don't have to be here. You know that, right? Just tell them—tell them what you know."

"I can't. I can't." His voice cracks with emotion. He starts to cry, wail.

"Why not? Why can't you tell them the truth? Who are you protecting?"

"Me! I'll be back on the streets if they release me."

"Isn't that a good thing? What you want?"

"You don't get it. He'll kill me, just like he did to Jamal."

"Who will?"

"We both saw him hide his stash. Jamal threatened to rat on 'im. I had no idea what he did to Jamal . . . until that cop told me. . . ." Heavy tears drip down from his eyes. "I need to stay here. Don't you get it?" He kicks at the wall. "Leave me the fuck alone. Get away from me." He cowers in the corner.

"Okay, okay, I get it." I feel the insides of my stomach coming up, and I *so* don't want to hurl. I manage to pull the hat off my head and turn it around.

Immediately, I hear a jangling of keys, the sound of heavy boots clomping down the hallway.

"Please, please don't say nothin'." Junior whimpers, mops up tears with his sleeve.

I crumple up the drawing of the claw, stuff it in my sweat-shirt pocket. "I won't. I promise you, Junior," I whisper back.

He looks up at me. "Wait. How d'you know my name?"

The sergeant approaches my cell, a tough expression firmly in place. "We have a few more questions for you." He unlocks the cage, pulls me out, cuffs my hands again, and drags me down the hall.

I glance back at Junior, see his dark eyes wide, like pools of black, thick ink, weighed down with . . .

Secrets and lies.

• • •

I lie on Daniels's office couch, take a sip of water, then place the cold plastic bottle on my forehead.

He pushes his desk chair over and sits. "How are you feeling?"

"My head still hurts, but not as bad." I roll over on my side and face him. "Hey, I'm sorry I couldn't get anything out of him."

"You didn't see anything? Nothing at all?"

I finger the bear claw sketch—stuff it down a little deeper in my sweatshirt pocket. *I've got to keep him safe—off the streets.* "No. He wouldn't make eye contact. I don't know; I'm not so sure he's innocent anymore."

"What? Why do you think that?"

"He's just meaner than I thought. Cold son of a bitch."

"But I saw you talking with him—"

"Yeah, yeah," I interrupt. "I tried to get him to talk, but he clammed up."

The lights in the room dim for a second, with a crack of lightning.

"Huh." Sergeant Daniels crosses over to the window . . . peers outside at the sudden rainstorm.

"What's going to happen to him now?"

"I don't know yet. I don't have much to work with—no murder weapon, no witnesses."

I sit up. "But the drugs . . . you found the pot on him, that has to be something."

"Yeah. Possession on school grounds, suspicion of distributing—a misdemeanor at best. We'll schedule a court hearing," he says, sifting through papers. He picks up the drawing of the tennis balls.

"Oh, that. . . . I'd forget about that sketch." I force a laugh. "Crazy, right? I bet it doesn't mean anything. I think it was because of my headache. There were, like, spots in my vision. I've been getting them with the migraines."

He walks toward me. "I shouldn't have had you down there. You sure you're okay?"

I wave him off. "I'm fine. No biggie. Just sorry I couldn't get you what you wanted. I better get home now. . . . Don't want to wig my parents out."

"I'll escort you out the back door."

"Nah, don't worry. I'll see myself out." I hitch up my jeans, roll them at the cuff. Pull off the sweatshirt. "Without my hat and hoodie I look kind of boring, don't you think? No one will notice me."

"Bea, you could never look boring."

I would savor that last comment if it weren't for the guilt I feel for fudging the truth. But the kid is petrified—no way I can ignore that. He knows something . . . a lot of something. Tennis balls, a bear claw. *What do they mean?* I have to find out, and without anyone knowing it came from Junior.

Without them thinking that he snitched.

6 days
5 hours
35 minutes

see Willa's car parked in Zac's driveway when I get home. She used to stop by my house, to say *hi* at least, when she came to see him, but now it's all about her obsession with him. I'm totally out of the picture.

Zac's little brother, a sophomore at Packard, hangs a huge banner along their fence in the rain. It reads: CORNELL (in big red letters). CONGRATULATIONS, ZACHARY! Jeremy's hair is soaked—stuck flat on his head—and he looks totally miserable.

Unbelievable. I know Willa got in, but Zac did, too? That bone-head? This really pisses me off.

Zac was the first person I met (sort of) when we moved to Ann Arbor. I saw him from way up high in the tree, that day we moved into our house. He was one of the boys playing football in the yard next door; he was taller and huskier than the rest, and I could tell, even then, that he was the neighbor-hood bully as he charged, chased down a boy half his size, and tackled him—smashing his little body into the lawn.

"That's not fair, Zac!" the little boy cried. "It's supposed to be touch football. That was the rule."

Zac ignored his cries and snatched the ball from the kid's puny arms, ran across the grass to the drive, raised his arms, and shouted, "Touchdown." Then he jackknifed the football onto the asphalt. It ricocheted off the drive and like a bullet, crashed through the front window of the house.

They all froze. I froze, too, along with the birds sitting in the tree. It was like all the oxygen was sucked out of the air. The front screen door squeaked open, and a woman came stomping out. She looked at the broken window, whirled around to the boys, and yelled, "Who did this? Who?"

They all stood there—tight-lipped—all stared at Zac.

He lowered his head; his voice cracked. "Jeremy did, Mom." Zac pointed to the scrawny kid. "I saw him. He did it."

"I did not, he did!" Jeremy sputtered, protested, "I can't believe you just said that, Zac."

The Zac kid started to cry big, phony fat tears, and then wailed, choked out, "Guh . . . you're such a liar, Jeremy. Mom told us to never lie. Fine. I'll take the heat for you." He skulked to his mom, head hung low, and tightly hugged her. "I'm sorry," he feigned. "I'll clean it up, and you can take it out of my allowance." His voice was muffled in the waist of her jeans.

The mom stuttered, stammered, and then we all watched her make the call, like a referee on the field, as she petted the thick, brown, sweaty mop of her older son's head. She then shouted the penalty: "Jeremy. You get in this house right now, young man, in your room. You're grounded for a week."

Jeremy whimpered, "But, Mom . . ."

"Don't *but Mom* me. Now! Did you hear me?"

His skinny shoulders slumped as he passed his big brother, walking toward the house, whining under his breath. The screen door squeaked open and slammed closed. The other kids scattered.

And there I was, sitting way up in the tree, getting my first big dose of suburban family dynamics, thinking . . . *the big brother is ratting on his little brother? Lying about it?* Even at six I knew it was obviously WRONG.

I wanted to jump down from the tree, right the wrong, knock on the door, and tell the mom the truth. But Zac, alone in the yard now, kind of snickered, high-fived the air, started toward his house, and then spotted me—caught me spying on him from the tree.

Our eyes locked, and he did that weird twitching thing with his jaw and then gave me the finger, pulled the back seam of his shorts out of his butt crack, and huffed inside his house.

He was a jerk then, and a bigger jerk now.

I pull over to the side of the road, roll down the window, and yell out to Jeremy, "How did he manage that?"

"I dunno. Beats me."

"Well, why are you putting up the banner, and not him?"

"What . . . you expect the king to do it in the rain? I'm just happy he'll be out of the house." He turns, walks to his front door—his shoulders slumping in defeat like they did twelve years ago in his front yard; like they probably did so many times in his life.

• • •

I fly up the stairs to my room before my mom sees my gangsta getup.

She calls out, "Bea . . . dinner in a half hour. Dad's coming home."

Dad's coming home? Huh. My dad hasn't been home for dinner in ages, ever since this dean job thing came up. "Okay, Mom."

My phone pings with a text:

BILLY: Stan the man's down w/a meet'n'greet w/u

I text back:

ME: Awesome! TY Billy☺

I jump on my bed, flatten out the crumpled sketch of the bear claw, and study it now that my head is free of pain, my eyes clear. Damn . . . this would make a wicked tattoo. *Huh. A tat . . . Junior had a few of them.*

I open my laptop, pulling the screen in close, and type in: *Bear Claw tattoo Ann Arbor*, and hit images.

A picture of a bakery pops up; a girl's racy (bordering on porn) Facebook page; Stan's the Man Tats tattoo parlor. I bookmark the site and then scroll down the page at dozens of images. And then I see it—the bear claw Junior was thinking about, what I saw in his eyes—the claw I drew. Primal, almost primitive. I click on *visit site* and it directs me to a YouTube video.

"I'm Coach Credos." The camera focuses in on a huge— I'm talking *gigantic*—Hispanic guy with a shaved, shiny head. His gapped-tooth smile is neatly tucked into a fleshy face on top of a heavily tattooed neck—black ink barbed-wire circles the collar of his shirt; a scary inked eye stares out over his Adam's apple.

He resembles a rabid shar-pei dog ready to bite. A heavy brow flaps over beady eyes—underneath, a tatted teardrop drips down his cheek. He's super macho—tacky, thick gold chains hang around his neck. He flexes his right bicep—as wide as it is long and tattooed with a bear claw, and he wears a skintight black T-shirt that has the same claw printed on the front.

Young teens, different races, male and female, seemingly wannabe rappers, are flinging gang-speak: "Wangsta gangsta's all fo' one. Wangsta gangsta's one fo' all." They show off, posing for the camera, competing with one another like a litter of hyper puppies.

And there he is in athletic gear—Junior, in the middle of

the pack, smiling, dancing, with happy eyes, so different than at the station—tossing off some hand signals and fist-bumping a white dude, having fun, looking happy.

The video cuts to a homeless shelter; they ladle out soup. Cuts to the gang cleaning, washing, and painting over graffiti on a train boxcar. *That's what Junior was talking about with, "I probably cleaned up your art."*

The video jumps to an outdoor track—in the middle of a race. A baton is handed off to Junior—the last leg in a relay. He crosses the finish line, and the clan runs up, huddles, high-fives him. They face the camera, sweaty, out of breath, and say in unison: "Make friends, not victims." A chick, edgy as all get-out—thick, black eyeliner, safety pins lining the lobes of one of her ears, silver hoops in her bottom lip—jumps on Junior's back.

Back to the coach: "You want a life? You in need of a family? You don't have to run down the wrong road." He jams his thumb into his chest. "Start running down my road. Credos Kidz—The Kodiak Kidz. We meet most afternoons, Skyline High. Four o'clock."

"Bea, now!" my mom yells from downstairs. "It's getting cold."

"Okay, okay!" I yell back. "One sec."

I change out of the baggy jeans and hoodie and back into my bell-bottoms, unpin the twists, pulling at the strands. I shake my head, and the coils kind of fly around freely—bouncing like little firework explosions. I line my eyes with chocolate brown pencil, apply mascara; with my hair out of my eyes, my eyes jump out, catlike. Fearless. *Dang. I like this look.*

The parents ordered in Chinese, and I stand at the kitchen counter stabbing prawns in a take-out carton, studying for my astronomy class. Mom and Dad sit at the table. They're bickering as usual. It's a hobby of theirs.

"I told you to tell them to hold the green pepper," Mom complains, spitting one out in her napkin.

"I did, Bella. They must have forgotten."

"I always check before I pay."

"Then I guess you should pick up the food from now on," he murmurs. "I thought you'd be happy I got home for dinner."

"What a treat. I should've put out the good china."

"Aren't you going to sit, Bea?" Dad asks, ignoring Mom's barb.

"I'm studying for an astronomy test, and it's easier up here on the counter with my book." I also don't want to be hit by a flying dumpling—you never know with them.

Dad's cell rings.

Mom gives him the evil eye. "Work I suppose?" She makes no attempt to hide her frustration, slamming her iced tea down on the table.

Dad answers abruptly. "I'll call you later, okay?" He hangs up.

Mom turns on me. "What's with your hair, Bea?"

Whoa . . . okay, that came out of nowhere. I swallow the shrimp with a little help from my Diet Coke. "I'm trying out a new style. Eva Marie did it. She's applying to cosmetology school, and I thought I'd let her practice on me." *And I wanted to have a gangsta look going on while I sat with a punk who confessed to murder in a holding cell this afternoon.*

Dad smiles. "I like it, Bella. Makes her eyes pop." He nods his head in sync with his chewing.

"I thought so, too, Dad. Thanks."

Mom fidgets, tops off her iced tea, pushes the starchy kernels around her plate with chopsticks, as if she's writing out a secret code.

Dad stops her hand. "You're not hungry?"

She pulls her hand away. "I'm just tired. You got home so late last night. I couldn't fall back to sleep."

"I'm sorry, Bella. The dinner with the provost went on longer than I thought."

"Uh-huh." She lifts her hair and clamps it in a high, messy bun. "I finally fell back to sleep about six, and slept in till . . . what?" Her pocketed phone *pings* with a text—she ignores it. "Was it after eleven, Bea? Is that when you came home?"

I'm outlining the constellation Serpens, labeling the stars in its tail, and look up at her question, thinking for a second about this morning's encounter, and with my pen on the paper, the letters *MC* end up on the tips of a northern hemisphere star.

MC? What does that mean? And then a dark, thick, bushy moustache appears on the mythological serpent handler's face, and I shut my eyes—no way I want anything else snapping in my head. I avoid, at all costs, drawing while making eye contact with my parents for exactly this reason. *TMI—I don't want to know their secrets.*

Dad tries to change the channel and singsongs, "I've got two girls with birthdays coming up this month. Two very important birthdays."

"Don't remind me," Mom mumbles.

"Turning forty is a wonderful thing, Bella."

"Really, Richard? Tell me about it, please. Impart your knowledge about what it's like being forty for a woman. I'd love to hear it."

Dad's face sags, and he obviously doesn't know what to do with that—doesn't want to touch it—and I don't blame him. He focuses on me. "So, what do you want to do for your special day, Bea?"

Get my own apartment. "Oh, I don't care. Not much, I guess."

"I know. How about we celebrate at the Gandy Dancer, at the train station? You love that restaurant . . . watching the trains chug in."

Watching me hopping on one, getting out of town. "Sure, sounds great, Dad."

"You used to get so excited when they barreled in—when you were little." He chuckles at the memory. "Sound good to you, Bella?"

She's gazing at the rain pounding at the window above the sink. The wind has picked up, and it's pouring down sideways, spitting at the window, leaving angry exclamation points. "What? Um, sure."

"Settled." Dad focuses on me. "Any college acceptances you've heard about?" He tries to hide a smile.

I knew this was coming. . . . "Well, Chris got into U of M. But of course you already know that, since it's your department."

Dad's smile grows as he slaps his hands on the table.

Mom jumps. "Jesus, Richard."

"It was hard keeping that from you." He walks behind me and squeezes my shoulders. "We're looking forward to having him in the art department."

"He's excited, too, Dad."

"How about Willa? Did she find out anything?" Mom asks.

"Yup. She did it. Her dream school—she got into Cornell."

"Ivy League, wow. Good for her." I can feel my dad's words scorch my back and his disappointment splatter against me like uncooked rice pellets.

"That's nice for Willa," Mom says.

"Yeah, and it seems Zac got in, too," I say.

"I saw the banner hanging on the fence when I drove by." My dad digs into my carton of shrimp.

"It blows my mind," I can't help adding.

"Why's that?"

"Because he's a bit of a moron. Not exactly the brightest bulb in the school. Guess they needed a two-hundred-pound wrestler at Cornell."

"I doubt that, Bea. It takes a lot more than being good at a sport to get into Cornell," Dad says, mouth full. "And, don't forget, his parents both graduated from there. A legacy applicant."

"Whatever. He aced the SAT and won't shut up about it."

"There you go," he punctuates. "That's quite a feat." My dad jump-shots the now empty Chinese carton across the kitchen. The orange sweet-and-sour sauce dribbles on the floor as the carton flies through the air and nails the trash can, successfully scoring two points.

"For chrisssake, Richard. Watch what you're doing." Mom jumps up, wrings out a sponge, and starts to wipe the spillage.

"He was just having fun, Mom. Chill. You're acting so jiggy-like."

"Fine—have fun." Mom throws the sponge at Dad. "And then clean up the fun." Her cell buzzes again in her pocket. This time she pulls it out, reads a text, and smiles.

"Who's that, Bella?" my dad asks, dutifully wiping up the orange goo on the floor. "And why do you get to answer at dinner when I can't?"

What, are they in junior high?

"Oh . . . it's about that job. You know, the mural in Bloom-field Hills." She takes her plate to the sink, scrapes the rest of her dinner into the garbage. "And it's *after* dinner now, by the way."

"You're not going to finish?" Dad puts his hand on the small of her back. She steps away from it.

"No, I'm feeling a little . . . jiggy-like." She darts her dark eyes at me. "I think I'm going to lie down upstairs for a bit."

I watch her climb the stairs, reading a message on her phone and smiling . . . for the second time today. *Weird.*

Dad's eyeing me, and I know why. I don't want to have to

list all the universities that everyone else got into—*everyone but his daughter.*

Wendell comes to the rescue, and texts:

WENDELL: r U coming to the 8pm meeting?

I close my textbook. "I've got a meeting tonight, Dad. I should get ready."

"Really? Your mother told me you missed the one in the morning, so you went to one after school."

"Oh, well, I kind of missed that one, too. I got suckered into helping Eva Marie—you know, with my hair, for her portfolio and shit. . . ."

He clears his throat.

"I mean, stuff."

He crosses to the sink. "You'll be getting your nine-month chip soon, right?" He flips on the faucet.

"Right." I bite my lip, and the memory of that night, the mukluk, kicks me in the stomach again.

"Dad?"

"Yes, baby?"

"I'm sorry I'm not going to college . . . if I've disappointed you."

His broad shoulders silhouette the window, and I see his reflection; see his face make the adjustment from honest disappointment to fatherly bullshit. "Oh, Bea, no. Don't think that," he says, collecting the dishes. "I'm not going to lie to you. I'd love to have you at school, especially my school. Would love to show you off. But I trust that you'll do just fine with whatever direction you decide to go. You've been through a lot. Your mother and I only want the best for you."

"Whatever direction?"

"Sure. Why? Do you have something in mind?"

"Well, I was thinking about getting a job after graduation," I boldly state.

He slings a towel over his shoulder. "But you already have a summer job. With your mother."

"I, um . . . I don't know how I feel about painting murals. It's not really my thing, you know?"

He nods. He thinks the same thing, I can see it in his eyes—he hates the murals. It's beneath the artistic persona that he proudly carries around with all his diplomas.

"But I'm afraid she'll get super pissed and flip out, if I don't help her out."

He wipes rice off the counter. "Well, why don't you look around, explore other possibilities."

"You'd be okay with that?"

"If you find something else that interests you, sure. I could always talk to your mom about it first, go at it from a different angle, and maybe lessen the blow."

I stand on my toes, reach up and over the counter, and hug him. "Oh, Dad, thanks. That means so much to me."

He pats my back. "And then perhaps you'll feel differently in the fall. It doesn't have to be U of M, you know. There's

Eastern, Kalamazoo, even Cranbrook Academy of Art—you could live at home, commute."

My heart sinks. I pull away from the hug—my feet fall flat on the floor. "But you didn't go to college—right away after high school. You took a few years off, right?"

Dad starts wiping the counter—again. "That's right, I did."

"Did you work?"

He wrings out the sponge. "I made money, yes."

"How? What'd you do?"

"Oh, just odd jobs here and there." He drapes the towel over the sink, walks over to me, and kisses the top of my head, just like he used to do when I was a little girl. The head that I'm sure he thinks *should* graduate from college—sporting the U of M blue and maize mortarboard. "I'd better see how your mom is doing." He walks out of the kitchen. "Have a good meeting, hon. I'd bring an umbrella, and be careful driving. It's slick out there."

I don't know the whole story—have never fully connected the dots. My dad is very private about his past, always has been, but from what he's said, what Mom's said, he grew up in the ghetto of Detroit, left home as a teen before he even graduated from high school, got his GED, and eventually applied and was accepted to an art school in Chicago. There he met my mom, knocked her up, had me, continued to study for years, leading up to his PhD, and landed the job at the University of Michigan.

Sounds simple, right?

Sounds like secrets and lies to me.

6 days
4 hours

The meeting is held at St. Anne's recreational hall, in the basement. We carry around our stories—all different circumstances that got us here together holding hands—but have one thing in common: the nasty, ugly beast of addiction.

My dad was right. I should be going on nine months and hate thinking about that night with Marcus. But I made good on my side of the deal—accomplishing the thirty/thirty for Sergeant Daniels, and he made good on his—not telling my parents about the slipup last November. And I've been coming back every week to St. Anne's.

Willa, now being sober, restructured the entire AA schedule with the same intensity she brings to everything. She complained that we needed a young persons' meeting and stood at the door like a bouncer, checking IDs, allowing everyone under twenty-five in the door. Those who were older had to meet in the upstairs choir loft. (Hah. . . . Sergeant Daniels wouldn't have made the cut.)

She took control; dumped out the brown, tar-tasting water and brought in coffee from Starbucks; decorated the hall for Christmas, Hanukkah, Kwanza, and baked cookies accordingly (so as to not exclude anyone) during the holidays; hosted a sparkling apple cider New Year's party complete with glitter-flecked hats and noisemakers; dipped strawberries in chocolate for Valentine's Day; pinched anyone not wearing green on St. Patrick's Day (me being one of them—green doesn't look good on me, what can I say?); and tonight she switched the sugar to salt on the coffee table in honor of April Fool's Day. And she is giggling her pert ass off watching the spit-takes.

"What the . . ." I almost hurl, spitting the yuck back in the Styrofoam cup.

"Ha ha ha ha ha," she singsongs. "I'm so good at this."

"What?" I wipe my tongue with a napkin.

"Fooling peeps."

"Yeah, well, we established that last fall." I chug a bottle of water. "Hey, Willa . . . did Zac really get into Cornell? Or is that a joke, too?"

She play slaps me—thinks I'm kidding. "It's amazingly cool, isn't it? We're already talking about getting a place together sophomore year." And then she does a little dance thingy as if she's swinging a hula hoop around her hips. "Oh my god, don't move. Here he comes. . . ."

Wendell heads over to us.

"Promise me"—she grabs my hand, whispering—"promise that you'll ask me to be your maid of honor at your wedding, okay? Promise me that."

"Willa, it's not like that, we aren't . . ."

"Well, he is." She leans forward, her blue eyes wide, two inches from mine. "I know. I sense it every time he looks at you. That's your husband, Bea. Your future."

My should. Mr. and Mrs. Should.

"Don't mess it up," she orders, kicking me in the shin.

"Hey, Bea, Willa." Wen fills a cup of coffee from the urn. He's about to pour from the sugar container.

I stop his hand. "Don't. It's salt."

Willa stomps her foot. "You blew it, Bea. You ruined it! Why do you always have to be so honest?" She huffs off.

That's a first . . . me being accused of being too honest.

Wendell sips his coffee. "Thanks, I guess?" He sweeps the back of his hand down the side of my face. "That's a new look for you—your hair—I like it."

"Yeah. Thanks."

I gaze into his amazing, "every-girl-wants-to-jump-your-bones-right-now-at-this-moment" eyes, and then break the stare. "Let's find a seat, hopefully without a whoopee cushion."

He laughs. *Of course he does. He does everything right. Even gets my jokes.*

Wendell is a freshman at Eastern Michigan University and

has been clean for a couple years. He's about the height of my dad—more than six feet—and kind of looks like a young Denzel, sexy overbite and all. His dad is Willa's dogs' vet, and Wendell, wanting to continue the family business, is studying veterinarian science. He's smart, handsome, sexy, and . . . really, um, nice. I don't know why that bothers me, but, yeah, he's nice.

We started out sitting across from one another (Willa thought it was more inviting, intimate—arranging the chairs in a circle), and I caught him staring at my legs in January when I was wearing a suede miniskirt and my chunky Doc Martens boots—his eyes caught in the fishnet of my stockings. My cleavage—it isn't much to brag about—but it drew him in in February with a low-cut forties cardigan, the top three buttons undone. March brought us sitting side by side, and if I wasn't mistaken, I caught him checking out my ass one night as I bent over to pick up my purse, when I was wearing my skinny jeans with three-inch platform shoes.

Willa begins the meeting, of course, announcing tonight's agenda, and Wendell leans over, smelling of fresh vanilla beans.

"You free after?"

"Sure."

Willa clears her throat, reprimanding us for interrupting her no doubt meticulously prepared speech, so I write in my Moleskine:

Cappuccinos at Rosie's?

He takes the book from me and writes:

My roommate is gone for the weekend.

He winks.

Oh, damn.

The last time I was in his dorm was when he invited me to a March Madness basketball game party. Wendell and his deadbeat roommate, Tom (I'm talking zombie-dead), had some buddies over. I went, even though I have zero interest in sports.

Well, his friends acted all dweeby and awkward after I took off my jean jacket. Maybe it was because I wore a black lacy bustier with low-rise jeans, highlighting the cubic zirconia stud pierced in my navel. It's not that I was trying to look like a tramp, but it was so friggin' hot in his dorm the last time I was there—not having a separate thermostat—and the thought of hanging around with his beer-drinking, rowdy buddies already had me in a flop sweat. . . . Hence the dated Madonna look.

Thankfully, Tom invited another chick, his girlfriend, Julie something. She was gorgeous. I mean, Christ, I had a girl crush the moment I set eyes on her. Everyone wanted to talk to her, be by her, touch her, smell her. Obviously used to all the fuss, she was totally at ease—like a Monet oil hanging in the same room with a bunch of velvet Elvises.

"Julie's studying anthropology of art at U of M," Tom boasted, basically drooling.

"That's cool. Bea's into art, too. And her dad's going to be the Dean of Fine Arts," Wendell bragged—trying to top him.

"Wen, that isn't definite." I dismissed him.

"Really?" This evidently piqued Julie's interest as she sat down on the floor, across from me. "What's his, I mean, your name?"

"Bea . . ." I started to say.

"Washington." Wendell finished for me, smiling like a cat with a bird in its mouth.

Something big happened in the basketball game, I guess a good thing, because the room exploded with cheers and high fives. I ignored the TV, opened my sketchbook, and started doodling, looking Julie's way, and wondered, *Why would this goddess date Tom, the oaf? Are they hooking up? Just friends?* I had to figure it out. It made no sense. He was like a bowl of oatmeal—before the raisins, pecan chips, and syrup—a cold clump of nothing.

I don't know why this was driving me crazy, but it was. So while the hoopla continued, I kept glancing up at her, you know, waiting to make eye contact—seeing if anything popped up. *And oh my friggin' god.* She wanted me. And not in a "friend" way. Okay, confession here . . . this didn't have anything to do with my flippin' skill. Not only did she make eye contact, she started flirting with me—licked her lips, twirled her hair, unbuttoned the top button of her top. Absolutely no drawing in the sketchbook involved.

I got a little nervous—never had a chick come on to me before—and suddenly had to pee. So I untangled my legs, then crawled up and over Wendell, who was sitting on the floor with me, staring at the TV. "Be right back, 'k?" My right leg had fallen asleep, but I managed to make it to the john.

I was standing at the sink, washing my hands, when Julie entered. She locked the door and jumped right in. A cannon-ball dive. "You're so hot," she said as she undid the rest of the buttons, exposing her bra—much more filled out than my bustier, and in ballet pink.

"Yeah, well, um, so are you," I lamely added—staring in the mirror at her pale skin and the blue veins spreading like a spiderweb through her set of ample twins.

"You ever been with a chick?" she teased—it actually sounded like a challenge.

"Um . . . no. Done a lot of kinky things, but not that."

"Too bad." She had the seduction act down as she slowly sidled up behind me and tickled her long slender fingers across my cleavage, down my belly, and played with the fake diamond in my navel. "I guess you're in for a treat."

I couldn't help but close my eyes as she touched me. I don't know if she heard my purring, but yes, she was definitely scratching the right place. And I felt things I never had before down . . . you know where.

You see, while with Marcus, I was high. Always. I don't think we ever didn't use, get blasted when together. So sex was . . . pretend sex. A faux fuck. Still naughty, forbidden, and that's what made it exciting, I guess. We were attracted to each other, for sure; but I was kind of numb. Numb from the brain down. In the two years that we were together, I'd never . . . peaked—had the big "O." I mean, I don't think so, anyway.

A loud knock on the door.

"Bea? Julie? You okay?" Tom asked.

"Yeah, Tom. Just a sec," Julie answered, taking a step back, and buttoned up her shirt.

"Can I ask you a question, Julie?"

"Shoot."

"Why are you with Tom, anyway? What's the story?"

She looked into the mirror and applied lipstick. "Duh, he's super rich. His dad is a partner at one of the top law firms in the state. I have to think of my future, you know—like a degree in anthropology is really going to get me anywhere? Oh, by the way . . . is your dad Richard Washington, the chair?"

"Yeah, he is." *Now I get it. . . . She's a user. Been there. Done that. Big time.*

She smiled at me in the mirror—the corners of her eyes crinkled up in a bad-girl way as she licked her crimson lips, spun me around, and wrote her phone number on my belly with the lipstick. "There's more here, if you want it. Let's hang out sometime." She unlocked the door, then turned back. "Hey, don't tell Tom about this—my little hobby, okay? The secret's between us?" She didn't wait for my answer and joined the boys in the sweaty man cave.

I bit my bottom lip and called Chris.

Me: You're not going to believe what just happened.

Chris: With you? Probably not.

Me: A chick just tried to pick me up. And it felt kind of good.

Chris: So, what you're telling me is you're a lesbian now? Bi?

Me: No. I'm not a lesbian or bi—I mean, not that there's anything wrong with it. I just can't seem to get it up for Wen.

Chris: Bea, I think that's what the guy says.

Me: I know. That's what pisses me off. It's crystal clear for you guys. When it's up, it's up. Staring you right in the face. It's not that way for a girl. It's so confusing.

Chris: Um . . .

Me: You're supposed to help me. You're my gay friend.

Chris: Is there a gay-friend handbook I'm not aware of?

Me: I don't know. But there should be.

Chris: Not that I don't want to help you, but maybe you should find a girlfriend to talk about this with?

Me: Well, I do have a number on my belly of a girl I could call.

Chris: What? You're not high, right?

Me: No, of course not. I wouldn't be feeling anything if I were.

"Bea?" Wendell knocked on the door. "Are you okay? What's going on?"

Me: I better go.

Chris: I'll look for that handbook.

Me: Love ya.

Chris: Love ya back.

"Yeah, I'm fine, Wen. Just a little tummy something," I said as I wiped Julie's number off my belly. (But not before I copied it in my phone.)

"She's nice, isn't she?" he asked as I joined him on the couch.

"Julie? Yeah. Really nice." I popped a pretzel in my mouth and gulped down a bottle of water—wanting to pour it over myself, to cool down.

The basketball game continued. It was a blowout, they said, so the party fizzled—everyone left (including Julie, with a smoldering, hot-as-hell wink for me), and there we were. Wendell and me. Alone in his bedroom, totally making out.

And again, I was faking, waiting for something—the tingle, the sensation experienced in the john with Julie, and sometimes, sort of, with . . . yeah, Sergeant Daniels.

But Wendell? Nada, nothing.

And I'm thinking the whole time we're at each other, humping and pawing: *Jesus, I'm crazy. He's so fine. Every girl I know would kill to be in my position . . . literally. He's got it going on—the looks, the personality, the smarts, and the smell: he really does smell like fresh vanilla beans—and I'm the one he picked. What's wrong with me?*

"Bea?" Wendell sat up on his bed. "Are you okay? You seem . . . distant."

"Oh, sorry."

"Am I rushing things? Going too fast for you?"

I jumped on that excuse like a hobo on a runaway train. "Yeah. That's it." I threw on my jean jacket. "I'm sorry, it's just, um, like you said . . . too soon."

So, that was the last time I was at his dorm, and now, back at Saint Anne's, his invitation hovers.

I respond, in writing:

Let's just do Rosie's for coffee, 'k?

Wendell pats my thigh and nods, writes:

I understand.

Shit. Why is he so nice?

6 days
55 minutes

What a trippy day. I'm lying in my bed, tired as hell, thinking about the crazy April Fool's Day I had.

The rainstorm is finally dying down, and the giant sycamore in the front yard of my house calls me over, waving in the breeze. Little did I know, the first time I climbed it, that that tree would be my fortress over the years. It's helped me quiet my mind, sort things through when I was bullied in grade school and rejected in middle school, and escape from my bedroom in high school. . . . Oh yeah, and protected me from the wrath of Zac.

I open my window. "Hey, girl. You enjoying spring? I like your new buds." I inhale, smelling the crisp, raw, moist air, and immediately sneeze. *Ugh.*

I grab a box of Kleenex, pull my desk chair over to the window, study the sky, sketch the almost full moon behind the dark purple clouds, and write the words *Sweet Dreams* using the letters as sparkling stars, creating my own constellation tattoo.

I close my eyes and imagine my future, my dreams, as an adult. *I picture a studio apartment in a city somewhere—not much furniture, but piles of colorful pillows scattered on a shiny parquet floor. I drape the large windows in something funky like burlap or jute, allowing the sunlight to filter in. Friends, neighbors—fellow artists and musicians—we discuss art over exotic tea and too many cups of strong black coffee. I sling a leopard pashmina shawl over a silky black camisole, and saunter over to work, to my own tattoo parlor—Thru Bea's Eyes.*

Jazz musicians jam on the corner. "Hey, Bea!" a sax player calls out. "Looking good tonight, babe!"

"Thanks, Joe!"

Chris and I meet up on weekends. He's totally out *now, and so happy. Mom and Dad visit. We laugh a lot—no drama—or maybe a little, but it's manageable drama. I talk my mom into getting a tat on her ankle—my design, a wicked-ass ram (her astrological sign), and my dad starts painting again. Our easels sit side by side. Hours drift away as we're absorbed in our art—until Dan calls, Dan Daniels, and we meet after work. We continue to see each other, and he stops treating me like a kid, and I stop treating him like an old fart, and it develops into something more, something . . .*

Knock. Knock. "Bea? Can I come in?"

My dream whooshes out the window, washes into the gutter, and down onto the wet lawn, forming a fantasy puddle that will evaporate, I'm sure, by morning.

Mom enters and hands me my astronomy book. "You left this on the kitchen counter. Thought you might need it."

"Oh, thanks." I take it from her and shut the window.

"How was the meeting?"

"It was okay."

She scrunches up her forehead. "What happened to the one after school? The same thing that happened to the one before school?"

Crap. "Um . . . like I said to Dad, Eva Marie needed my help—you know, with her portfolio."

She sits on the edge of my bed. "Bea, is there anything we need to worry about?"

I laugh. "All you do is worry. You need more?"

Her eyes narrow.

"Mom, I've just got a lot going on, with school, AA, Wendell . . ." *A murder case.*

"Uh-huh." Eye contact still zeroing in.

I sit at my desk, open my astronomy book, and fake a yawn. She stays seated on my bed—not picking up the cue that it's time to leave. "I'd better get some more studying done before I hit the sack."

She doesn't move.

"Is there something you need, Mom?"

"Are you going to keep your hair in twists?"

"What? I was thinking about it, yeah. Why?"

"Well, I was tossing around ideas about your birthday present and thought maybe you'd like to have your hair relaxed . . . while you're growing it out. We could do a mother/ daughter day at the salon. How does that sound?"

I pull at a coil. "I don't know. I don't think so. I like my hair like this. It feels good. True to me."

She shrugs. "It's a little . . . ethnic-looking."

I whip around and face her. "Ethnic? You mean black?"

She fluffs a pillow that doesn't need fluffing. "You're not *just*—"

"I know. I get it, Mom. I'm African American *and* Italian American. But, honestly, when people look at me . . . what they see is that I'm black."

The fluff of the pillow morphs into a punch. "Well, that hairstyle doesn't help."

She blinks a couple times, telling me she knows she went too far.

"Are you kidding me?" I cross to my closet and grab a sweatshirt. It's suddenly very chilly in here. "Wow. I'm sorry I'm so disappointing. I'm sorry if I resemble Dad more than you."

"Oh, Bea. You're beautiful. You know I think that."

"You used to. You had no problem back in the day with my *ethnicity* as you put it. You're the one who bought me my first black Barbie doll, remember?"

She stands, smoothing my bedspread where she was sitting because there's no way she can smooth the kink out of my hair. "I'm sorry I brought it up. I thought it would be fun to go to the salon with you. It seems like we haven't been connecting lately."

"That's for sure," I mumble.

And then she basically remakes my bed. Pillows thrown, quilt on the ground. She shoots the sheet up high into the air, and it parachutes down, the same place it friggin' was.

"Mom. Stop making the bed."

She does. Her eyes are unusually sad. And I think I know why: guilt. The only obvious gene that Mom's passed down to me (besides the faint moustache that I have to wax every two weeks or so—oh yeah, and my short-fuse temper) is the addict gene. Yup. Mom's been sober for more than ten years now. I don't know the whole story—don't know if I want to know—what her screwups were. I sort of remember some messes when I was a little girl—deep down, pushed away memories. But she obviously fucked up enough to quit drinking. Just like her little girl.

"It's late. I have to get up early for work." She walks to the door. "Mr. Connelly is expecting me at eight."

"Mr. Connelly? You have to call your boss Mr.?"

"Well, it's Mike, Michael, but yeah, I like to keep it professional. Good night, Bea. Sweet dreams." She closes the door.

Sweet dreams? Not happening. I rip out the page of the moon-and-stars tattoo—crumble it up. Open and then throw it out the window, hoping it drowns in the puddle with the fantasy.

I plop down on my bed and put a pillow over my face. *What am I doing? Dreaming? Fantasizing. I'm only setting myself up for disappointment. . . . Everything is already mapped out. Just let it be.*

Let it be.

Let it Bea . . .

I jump up—sit upright on my bed. *Mike Connelly . . . MC. Oh my god, her client, Mike Connelly—that's who she was thinking of, who she was texting.*

4 days
12 hours
45 minutes

"Okay, class." Mr. Pogen hands out tests. "This is our last quiz before the final exam next month. Take your time, use your notes, ask your fellow classmates. This will serve as your study sheet for the final. I promise you, no surprises. It's all here."

I love Mr. Pogen, as does every other senior. Astronomy, specifically the Sea of Tranquility, is the most popular class last semester—rarely skipped, even though senioritis runs through the halls like rabid rats. The class is jam-packed with over fifty students, sitting everywhere from the floor to windowsills— partly because the class is an easy A, but mostly because Mr. Pogen is the coolest dude on the whole planet, probably the whole solar system.

I choose to sit on the floor in the corner of the room. Knowing I'll have to put a pen to paper, I face away from the other students and toward the bookcase. Chris gets it, of course, and joins me—so it doesn't seem too weird.

My stupid *skill* is a real hassle at school. I found out the hard way and know some stuff about the teachers that I really don't want to know. So I try to never hold a pen in my classes. I explained that I'm an auditory learner and record lectures on my phone. I thought it was pretty clever of me, and most of the teachers were fine with it. I mean, there's a lot more crap happening in their classrooms that they should be worrying about rather than a student recording what they're saying. But somebody complained to Principal Chump Nathanson. He tried to stop me, threatened to take my phone, but I'm acing every class, so he didn't have much ground to stand on and had to drop it.

Pencils scratching, whispering, pages turning—everyone's engaged. I'm drawing, labeling the fire constellations—the stars in the sword, flame, and the snake—when the door slams open, and in walks another snake: Zac.

"You're late." Mr. Pogen calmly states the obvious.

"Like I really need this class." Zac snickers, looks around as if seeking validation. Nobody pays attention to him. He tries again. "You know, like, 'cause I got into Cornell."

What an ass.

"Congratulations!" Mr. Pogen responds with genuine enthusiasm. "You're very lucky. I'm sure the stars were aligned accordingly when you took the SAT."

"Whatta you mean by that?" Zac's face gets all splotchy red.

And then the twitch thing happens—big time. His head jerks to the left, and he spots me sitting on the floor. Our eyes lock, and (*oh, no, no, no, no, please no*) . . . pencil to paper, something starts crawling in, scraggly lines, strands of hair, forming a triangle on a chin—what looks like a beard or a goatee.

"Mr. Posen?" Billy Weisman jumps off the windowsill with an unlit cigarette in his mouth. "I gotta take a leak."

"Go right ahead, Billy."

Billy passes Zac on the way out of the room, shoves his shoulder into him, and mimes a zipper closing on his mouth— does it superfast.

No. It can't be. I look back down at the scratches on the paper. *Billy's soul patch? Holy crap, I drew his goatee! Did he take the test for Zac? No way. He wouldn't have, couldn't have. . . . Could he have?*

My phone buzzes with a text from Daniels:

DANIELS: usual place. 4.

4 days
8 hours
48 minutes

make my way down the gully. The rain has stopped for the time being, but my red Converse high-tops and the bottom of my long, tie-dyed jersey maxi skirt gets soaked. (Chris and I had spent one lazy Saturday afternoon tie-dyeing clothes—we were so proud of ourselves until my mom threw a hissy fit because the indigo-blue dye also tie-dyed the dryer. The drum is still blue to this day.)

I crawl through the window—not easy with the skirt, but I wasn't planning on coming here. He's standing, waiting for me, wearing a green-checked button-down shirt, kind of nerdy-looking, but it makes the irises of his eyes stand out like two lime-flavored lollipops, and yes, I have the urge to lick them.

"What's up? Everything okay?"

"We made a major bust at Skyline High yesterday afternoon."

"Really? Wow. What happened?"

"In the middle of the night it popped into my head—"

"Nice to hear someone else has things popping in his head."
I walk past him and plop my bag down on the bench.

"I kept thinking about the tennis balls you drew out of
that kid."

I whip around. "What? No, no . . . I told you that sketch
meant nothing." *Shit. I didn't have time to check it out yet.*

"But they did, Bea—you nailed it again. I looked into it a
little more—brought in the narcs again, but this time with the
help of a drug-sniffing dog. Searched the whole school. The
scent lead them to an old shed behind the gym, filled with
discarded sports equipment. And in the corner, a netted bag
with dozens of tennis balls slit and stuffed, packed with drugs—
cocaine, acid, pot. Can you believe it? It was a major bust, Bea.
Someone was literally rolling the goods." He chuckles.

I don't. *Oh my god. They're going to think Junior snitched. Act
cool, breathe.* I sit on the bench. "Okay, so now you have more
evidence? To keep him locked away for a long time, right?"
That will keep him off the streets—keep him safe. "I knew he was
guilty; I told you that."

"Yeah, that bust would've been enough to hold him, but . . ."
Daniels looks down. "There's something else." He crouches
in front of me, puts his hands on my knees. "There was an
incident."

My stomach jolts. "What? What happened?"

"Junior—he was shot."

"What?"

"He's in surgery at St. Joseph's. They don't know if he'll make it."

I jump up, pace the dusty room, squeezing my head between my hands. *No, no, no. This can't be happening.* My eyes burn; my breath is held tightly inside my chest. "But, but . . . how did it happen? He was in custody." My voice sounds like it's outside of my body—coming from somewhere, somebody else.

"I couldn't keep him. The sentencing hearing for the pot was scheduled for next week. . . . He was free to go."

"What? You let him walk out? No protection?"

"I had to. There was nothing we could do. He was targeted, ambushed right outside his house last night after he was dropped off—someone wanted him dead, Bea."

"So it was after the bust at Skyline?"

"Yeah. A few hours later."

Fuck! "Who picked him up?"

"His coach—they call him Credos. He's a good man, cares about the kids on his team—keeps them out of trouble, off the streets."

I think of the gruff face on the YouTube video.

"This hit him hard, the coach. He's a mess. Says he took Junior to his house, didn't even get halfway down the block when he heard a gunshot. He was already down—hit in the temple. No one saw anything, it happened so fast."

I grab my purse off the bench. "I've got to get out of here." I rush to the window.

"Bea." He puts his hands on my shoulder. "What's wrong? I thought you'd be pleased about what you drew—what we found."

I push his hands off. "Pleased about someone getting shot?"

"I hate to say it, but it was inevitable. His whole family has been involved with gangs. I think you were right. Junior could have been dealing, could have killed Jamal. I have to admit maybe I was wrong about him."

I throw my sketchbook on the floor. "I'm not doing this anymore . . . this drawing shit. No more." I push at the plywood and climb out the window.

Daniels is fast after me. "Bea, stop. What's going on?"

I forge ahead, run down the hill, slip in my sneakers, and fall on my butt on the wet grass. The homeless man is hanging his wet socks on the branches of a scraggly sapling at the bank of the river, his box standing upended, soaked. He walks toward me, holds out his hand.

I wipe my eyes, pull out my wallet, and hand him a couple bucks. "It's all I have."

He waves it off. "No. No. I just wanted to help you up."

I take his hand, and he pulls me off the wet ground. "Are you okay?" he asks.

"No, I'm not okay." I take off running—cross the bridge—tears flowing. *He knew he'd be hurt, and I'm the one who ratted on him. It was because of me that he was hit. I'm the snitch.*

4 days
7 hours
50 minutes

I drive straight over to Skyline High, to the Kodiak Kidz team practice, and immediately take note of a couple police cars in the parking lot. Damn. They're keeping an eye on the place, and one of them is Detective Cole, leaning against his car, laughing his stupid cackle.

I for sure don't want him to recognize me and figure I'd better get my gangsta-look going. So I tug Billy's baseball cap over my twists, tuck them in, and even though it's warm—a humid sixty-something degrees—I pull on the heavy, baggy sweatpants under my skirt, slip the skirt off, and throw on Chris's red, loose pullover hoodie.

I look at myself in the rearview mirror. My allergies are jacked up—my eyes have been tearing since meeting with Daniels, so my eye makeup is nonexistent. The inside of my nostrils feels inflamed as hell, like the little hairs are pinpricks—scratching, tickling, and stirring up a massive amount of gunk.

Sweat beads above my lip. I wipe my face with a red bandana and then tuck it in my sweatpants pocket.

It's a little after four, and the athletic field below is bustling with activity. Various teams are working out, practicing— cheerleaders perfect a pyramid, pole-vaulters vault, runners sprint on the track. *Jocks.* Never understood them, never will. I stink at sports, was humiliated in fourth grade when I couldn't do a headstand in PE. It seems really lame right now, thinking back on it, but when you're nine years old and every other girl around you can pop her long legs up in the air like *what's the big deal?* and you can't, it sucks.

I spot what I know *has* to be the Kodiak Kidz, gathered under the goalpost, all wearing black T-shirts—with an imprint of a bear's claw slapped on the front.

I lope across the clay-red rubberized track over to a punky-looking, skinny kid. He's shorter than me, maybe a hundred pounds. His dull brown hair is buzzed on the sides, creating a mousy mohawk. He licks both of his palms and slicks back the sides of his head. Pimples dot his sweaty face. "Yo," he says, in a high, tinny voice. "Wazzup?"

"You in the Kodiak Kidz?"

"Yup. The name's Johnny." He fist-bumps me.

"Hey, I'm Bea. Where's the coach?"

He points across the track at the shar-pei–looking man from the video. "Over there." He gestures like he's holding an upside-down pistol, trying *so* hard to be cool.

"Okay. Thanks." I have no idea what I'll ask the coach, no

plan in my head—I only know that I have to start with him. He had to have seen something, someone when he drove Junior home. I jog across the damp grass and am totally out of breath by the time I get to the other side.

"Excuse me, sir?" I blow my nose with the bandana as snot rolls in like the tide and sludges down.

He's timing a chick running around the track. I recognize her as the safety-pin girl from the video. Her cutoff shorts ride up her cheeks. Her long, jet-black hair streams behind her as she pumps her arms like a machine and shoots around the oval like the devil. A pole-vaulter stops mid-vault to gawk; she winks at him. *Winks? How does she have enough energy to wink? I'm exhausted just watching her.* He totally misses his mark and falls flat on the padded surface, the pole falling on top of him. His teammates razz him. She whizzes past, and the coach's stopwatch clicks.

"Four seconds slower, Reyna. Twenty-five push-ups. And not girl-style."

"Awww . . . come on, Coach." She leans on her knees, panting.

"Now. And keep your eyes on the track next time, not the boys."

She mumbles an obscenity, falls to the ground, and starts pumping.

Another girl cracks up, slaps her thigh. She's just as edgy-looking as Reyna, but instead of safety pins in her earlobes, she wears tiny skull posts. Her lips are caked with black lipstick, matching the chipped black polish on her fingernails.

"You shut your trap, Roxanne. Or you'll be down on the ground with her."

I clear my throat. "Uh, sir? Coach Credos?"

He finally pivots around and peers at me. His eyes are little slits under a sweaty brow. Wide nose. Wide neck. Everything about him is wide. He leans in, two inches from my face. "I don't know who the hell you are, but I never want you to talk to me when I have this timer in my hand. You got that?" His breath smells of stale booze.

This is the guy Sergeant Daniels says is so good?

I forge ahead. "I came here to ask you about—"

"Give me a lap," he orders, snapping his fingers.

"What?"

"You hard of hearing?" he growls.

Holy shit, he's a mean son of a bitch.

He clicks the stopwatch, and I jump—start running around the track, as ordered. I immediately feel my right heel forming a ripe, fresh blister. *Damn.* I bought these high-tops to be a fashion statement, not to be friggin' exercised in.

I try to get my mind off the sharp, rubbing pain developing on my heel, when a side stitch starts to stab through a rib on my right side. I broke that rib last year when I was totally messed up. Kind of the worst night of my life—don't really want to think about it.

I pass the cheerleaders, now flinging their pom-poms around. I'm about to die, right in front of their eyes. *How sad if a cheerleader is the last thing I see in my life.* I start to slow, consider walking, thinking about how stupid I am. *I mean, what am I doing? What am I expecting to find? Like someone's going to pass me a note telling me who set up Junior? Who killed the kid in the river? The coach is suddenly going to remember he saw the shooter?*

And just as I'm about to throw in the towel and collapse, a buff dude with a ponytail burns past me, ripping down lane two on the track. I am downwind of him, and the smell of sexy boy-man sweat wafts my way, keeping me upright and moving. I surprise myself with a surge as I concentrate on the set of firm, high, rock-hard buttocks in front of me.

My lungs burn as I turn the bend. And I feel every cigarette I smoked the past year coming up, grabbing ahold of my neck, shaking and choking, strangling me. A thick goober-clump of snot forms in the back of my throat, and suddenly it feels as if I can't breathe. I stumble to the grass on the field, dodging runners, and kneel, gasping for air.

"Get your wimpy, sick ass off the ground!" the coach yells.

I pray that I'm not the one he's yelling at. But I am— duh—so I manage to stand and lope around limping, pitifully finishing the oval, not wanting to pass out from the lack of oxygen that's been sucked out of my brain, leeched from my body.

I practically fall, and crouch at the coach's feet as he clicks the stopwatch, look up at him, and flinch at the maniacal expression on his face. Then I hoist myself up, placing my hands on my knees, and wipe my nose.

The coach bends down, whispers, grossly spitting, "Do you know you just broke a record? Do you?"

I can't speak, so I stupidly shake my head.

"You won the SLOWEST LIMP-DICK RECORD I'VE EVER TIMED!" he shouts.

Safety-pin girl, Reyna, laughs her ass off.

"Shut up, Reyna," the coach barks.

She immediately stops, places her hand on her hip, gives me the evil eye.

"You a smoker?" the coach asks, attention back on me.

I nod, coughing.

"Well, that's the first thing that has to go. And believe me, I'll know. *You'll* know when you drag your ass around the track. You want to be here, with us? You quit. Today. Right now."

Wait . . . does he think I'm trying out for the team?

"And no drugs, no alcohol. Did you hear me?"

Huh. This may work. If I joined, hung out with them a little . . . maybe I'd get some answers—or at least clues. Someone has to know something.

"Stand up," he orders. "Look at me."

I do.

"Your eyes are all red. You using?"

"No." I try to catch my breath. "Allergies."

"I can't hear you!" he yells in my ear.

"Allergies, I said. They itch like crazy," I muster out.

"Mumbling? Forget about it. I don't take mumbling. You stand up straight, look me in the eye, and articulate your words. Like you actually have an IQ. You got that?"

I do as he says.

"Any muscles under that hoodie? Take it off, let me see your guns—see what I have to work with." He reaches out.

I instinctively swat his arm away from mine. "Don't touch me."

"What did you say?"

"I said don't touch me."

"Who the hell do you think you are?"

I breathe in deeply, thinking these will likely be my last words—I better make them good. "I don't *think* I'm anybody. I *know* who I am. My name's Bea."

"B? What's that short for? Where's your turf?" he clips back.

"Chelsea." I make it up.

"What's with all the red you're wearing? You in a gang?"

Damn. I didn't think through the gang-color thing. "Nah, no way." I shrug. "I'm just wandering. Looking for somethin' more."

He circles, checks me out, nodding. "I like your balls, B."

Balls? Does he think I'm a guy?

Mohawk Johnny snickers at something on the sidelines, covering his mouth with his hand, his knees bent and knocked together. *Yeah, I guess I do look more butch than he does. With his rosy-colored cheeks, a little mascara, a short tight dress in a peachy color? He'd be in the running for Packard High's next homecoming queen.*

"You're a little touchy, but that's okay—it'll make you fast off the start. But if you're in the game, no drugs, no cancer sticks, no taggin' action. No other homies but us. And believe me, I'll know. As soon as you can't make eye contact, fail a pee test, I'll know you're up to somethin'."

"I'm clean."

"You willing to do a pee test?"

I nod. *Yay. Finally, something I'm good at.*

"Okay, then, after practice." He claps his hands. "Everyone, on the ground. Stretch-out time."

The team scatters on the grass. The runner with the sexy ass that managed to drag me around the track sits down next to me. I now recognize his face from the video; he was the guy horsing around with Junior. His long, sandy brown hair, tied loosely in a ponytail, falls into his tiger-yellow eyes. He reaches for his toes, stretching his "white-as-seashell" legs covered in a beige fluff of fur. "Hey, I'm Archie."

"Hey, I'm Bea." It's now or never. "Junior says hi." I dive in.

Archie sits up. "Say what?"

"Yeah. I met him in the cage the other day. He told me about the Kodiak Kidz—thought I should check you out."

"What are you talkin' about? Where d'you see him?"

"I was pulled in for taggin'. Lame stuff. I don't know what he was in for, but he's a cool dude. . . . You a friend?"

He suddenly tears up, tucks his knee up to his chest. "Yeah. We're best buds." He wipes his eyes. "You heard what happened, right?"

"No. What?"

"The coach picked him up yesterday from the police station, brought him home. He was hit. Shot in the head."

"You're shitting me?"

"No."

"Oh my god." I cross my right elbow around my left arm (mimicking what Reyna's doing), pulling at it, stretching my shoulder out. "Is he okay?" I almost forget to ask.

"In the hospital. That's all I know—all that the coach told us when we got here today." Archie lowers his eyes. "Hell. I wish I could go see him, but the coach says he's in surgery. Said we'd all go tomorrow . . . if he makes it."

"Damn, that's heavy shit."

Johnny walks up, plops down on the turf. "What you guys jawin' on about?"

"Junior," Archie answers.

"I just met 'im the other day," I say. "He's the one who told me to come here—check you guys out."

"You know what happened?" Johnny asks, kind of whispering.

"Yeah, Archie told me."

Johnny shakes his head. "First Jamal, and now Junior."

"Jamal? Who's that? What happened to him?" I ask, playing dumb.

"You musta heard about it—it was all over the news the last couple days. . . . He was dragged out of the river Monday. Shot in the chest—went right through his heart."

"Oh, man. Was he part of the team?"

Archie tightens the laces on his shoes. "In and out. Couldn't stay clean."

"You know, Junior never told me. . . . What was he busted for? Was he using?" I ask.

Johnny leans in, whispers again. "Well, an undercover found a shitload of weed in his bag."

Archie stands. "But no way—*no way*—that was his, Johnny. Someone planted it. Everyone knows Junior was clean."

"Shhh . . . the coach is coming." Johnny jumps up. "He doesn't want us talking about any of it—spreading rumors."

The coach hands me a couple forms. "Fill this first page out. You'll need to get your parents or guardians to sign the rest."

I cross over to the metal bleachers and sit. Warmed by the hot sun, I feel the heat through my sweats, and . . . *Oh, hell. I think I started my period. Unreal.*

"Okay, everybody, let's gather around." The coach corrals the team into a huddle. Roxanne grabs Archie's hand. Reyna shoves her away and takes it herself. The coach squeezes little Johnny's hand, and the kid winces in pain. "Please, kneel." They do, and bow their heads. "We thank you, Lord Jesus Christ, for giving us a future, taking control of the steps we make around the track of life, keeping us strong, helping us make the right decisions. Thank you for giving us a second chance to do good, giving us the strength to stay clean. . . ." The coach gazes up to the sky.

I rudely sneeze. He glances over at me.

And it plops in my head like a brick. *Thump.* I flip the paper over and scratch it out with the pencil. No headache this time, not much of any sensation. I draw a rectangle, mottled and pockmarked—it looks like a lava rock, a pumice stone.

"Thank you, Lord. Amen," the coach finishes.

"Amen," they all repeat, and then cross themselves.

"Okay, now group hug." He waves me over. "Come on over here, B."

I do and am suddenly smooshed between a mohawk and safety pins.

"Hey, Archie," the coach calls out, "take him to the locker room, give him a cup."

What? The guys' locker room? Is he joking? But there's no smile on the coach's face.

"You pass the test? I'll see you here next practice. You run like a wimp, but I'll give you a second chance to prove yourself. That's what I'm all about, what we're all about—the second-chance gang. Get yourself some running shoes; those high-tops are for girls. What'd you say B stood for?"

Gulp. "Boy. They call me boy."

"And wear shorts, trash the hoodie—you look like a delinquent—and if you're lucky, we'll let you join the clan."

I follow Archie into Skyline's gymnasium. It's even bigger

than Packard's, and it certainly competes with the amount of elephant-size felt banners hanging from the two-story walls.

A girls' basketball team is in practice; their sneakers squeak on the shiny wood floor. Archie stops to flirt with one of the players. "You go ahead," he says to me. "I'll catch up with you."

I approach the locker-room doors, get a whiff of chlorine, surmising that there must be a pool somewhere nearby, and then see a couple of dripping, slick-haired girls with towels wrapped around their bodies. I'm about to follow them, when Archie comes up from behind me, shrugs past me. "Well, you going in, or what?"

"Uh, I don't know . . ."

He swings open the door to the guys' locker room, and I enter.

Someone—with his back to me, thank god—is pissing in the urinal. I shoot my eyes down at the tile floor and count the ugly turquoise squares lined with jagged grout.

Archie leans up against a row of gunmetal-gray lockers and releases his ponytail.

Yes, I'm now feeling total hair envy.

"The coach will assign you one of these"—he flicks at a locker. "You put all your crap in when you get here, like your Pokémon backpack." He laughs. "How old are you, anyway?" He doesn't wait for my answer. "You look ten. You even reach puberty yet?"

I don't know whether to be flattered or insulted that he didn't notice my faint moustache.

"And never be late. Automatic fifty push-ups—with his foot on your back. And it isn't fun, believe me."

"He's a real ball buster, huh? He treat everyone that way?"

"If you screw up, yeah." He slips his shoes off, tossing them in the locker, and then slams it shut. "Speaking of screwups . . ."

Johnny walks up and Archie suddenly whips a towel at him and *thwaps* him in the head. "You rank, dude. Get in the shower. You're killin' me."

"Fuck you, Arch. You smell like yo mutha's asshole."

Archie grabs the neckline of Johnny's shirt and pulls him in close. "You say anymore shit, and I'll waterboard you in the crapper. Smother your face in feces, you hear that?"

Johnny whacks his hand away. "Then I'll cut the balls off your mama's baby daddy."

They get rough with each other—really rough. Slapping at each other, Archie gets Johnny into a standing full nelson. Johnny responds by kneeing Archie in the balls. I can't tell if it's a for-real fight, or if it's just boy-play. Regardless, I'm very happy to be a girl at the moment—standing in a locker room, about to pee in a urinal.

"You hitting the showers, or what?" the coach's voice shouts out.

Archie and Johnny disentangle. Archie points to a urinal, pushes his hair out of his eyes. "Take a whiz." The cups are on the shelf.

Okay, now what? "Um, I gotta shit."

He flings his arms up into the air. "Oh man, the stalls are around the corner." He points. "But if you think you're going to dilute your piss with toilet water? Forget about it. The coach puts a chemical in the cup. He'll know. And then you're a goner."

"No, I really have to take a dump."

"Whatever." He pulls his T-shirt off. A fork-tongued serpent tattoo covers the defined muscles of his back.

"Nice tat." *Nice everything.*

"Thanks. My design." He bends over, unlaces his shoes.

"You into art?"

"Hell, yeah. Helps keep me straight edge—clean—ya know what I mean?"

"I do. I draw, too . . . thinking about getting into inking."

"No shit? You'll have to show me your stuff sometime. Junior was into it, too. . . . We did some crazy tags back in the day." He starts pulling his shorts down and bares the tight ass cheeks that got me around the oval.

I scuttle over to one of the stalls. Yup, I started my period. I rifle through my backpack and thankfully find a tampon. I write the letter *B* (for *Boy*) on the cup and place it under the stream of urine. I happen to be an expert at this, unfortunately. Did a lot of peeing in the cup—at the rehab, at home for my parents. I know how to point, aim, shoot, and give them what they want.

I leave the stall and almost run right into the coach.

"Boy. That your sample?"

I nod and hand him the cup.

"If it's dirty, don't even think of coming back here. Otherwise, we'll see you on Monday."

I debate whether or not to ask him about Junior—what he saw—but I'm not given the chance, as he abruptly marches away.

3 days
16 hours

My alarm goes off at eight—a gruesome hour on a Saturday. I groan and sit up, attempt to swing my legs around, when suddenly, extremely rude, aching pains shoot through every muscle, tendon, ligament, screaming at me, *What the hell did you do to us? Huh? Running? Are you nuts? We don't run. You're going to pay for it today!*

I brush my teeth then limp down the stairs in my "still-warm-with-sleep" plaid flannel pajama bottoms tucked into a pair of UGG boots (the only shoes that don't irritate the now-oozing blister on my heel), a baggy U of M T-shirt, and a bandana tied around the twists—the twists my mom hates, the twists that make me look *ethnic*.

She's standing at the counter, sipping coffee, reading the newspaper. "Why are you up so early? It's Saturday."

"I thought I'd help you with the mural in Bloomfield Hills."

She arches a brow.

I pull out a carton of orange juice from the fridge. "You know, learn the trade . . . so I can help you out this summer." *Gag*.

"Bea. You don't have to—"

"I know I don't have to," I interrupt. "But I want to. I want to see what you do, how you deal with your clients." *Like Mike Connelly*.

She folds the newspaper. "Oh, okay. But I'm leaving in fifteen. You'll have to get dressed."

I look down at my ensemble. "I am dressed."

Mom chokes on her coffee. "Oh, for chrissakes, Bea. Really? Your pajamas?"

"Just the bottoms. I'm comfortable, and I won't care if I get paint on anything. But I did brush my teeth." I shoot her a sassy smile and down the glass of juice.

"There has to be something else you can wear."

"You don't understand. My clothes are special to me. Everything hanging in my closet has a story . . . a history. And if it doesn't yet, it will, believe me."

I join her at the counter and pour myself a bowl of cereal. She shifts from one foot to the other, her hand tucked in her back pocket of her . . . "Get out. Are those new jeans, Mom? Turn around—are they Sevens?"

"Uh-huh," she flatly answers and keeps reading, pretending that I'm not boring a hole in her skull with my eyes.

I'm not letting her get off that easy. No way. If I were to buy—or even ask to buy—a pair of designer jeans (not that I would want to), no way would my mom say yes. *That's frivolous, Bea. Over a hundred bucks for a pair of pants? Ridiculous.*

She knows she's in trouble, and puts the paper down, sips at her coffee. "What? What's wrong with them?"

"Nothing. But kind of low-cut for a mom, don't cha think?"

The paper's thrown in the recycling bin. "You think I should wear the high elastic-waist kind, is that it? Now that I'm turning forty?"

"No. Jeez. I wouldn't be caught dead with you if you did."

"So your mom feels a little stylish; what's the problem?"

"Where are the overalls you normally wear?"

"They're in the wash."

"Well, that's perfect. They're already dirty."

She growls. "Bea. Stop. Okay? I want to look . . . nice. This is Bloomfield Hills we're talking about."

"Oh, paint doesn't stain fancy pants there, I see."

Mom sighs in frustration.

"Who are you trying to impress, anyway? A six-year-old?" *A Mike Connelly?*

"Her name is Alanna, and she's not six, she's ten."

"Oh, well, that makes sense now. I should change, too." I slurp up the milk in the bowl.

Mom grabs her purse, then dumps her mug in the sink. "Put your coffee in a travel cup. We've got to go. I'm late already, with all this . . . banter."

"You're the one who started the battle of the clothes, not

me. By the way, why don't you give me the address? I'll meet you there. I have some errands to do." *Like find a pair of decent running shoes for track practice.*

She rolls her eyes. "It's never easy with you." She writes down the address.

"Tell the guard at the gate you're meeting me. Park on the street and buzz when you get there."

"The guard at the gate? Where are we going, Buckingham Palace? Maybe *I* should change into my sexy jeans."

She mumbles something evil in Italian as she walks into the garage.

• • •

I pick up a pair of slightly-used Adidas and shiny, yellow athletic shorts—long, down to my knees (like the guys are wearing them now); they're a little big in the waist, but a safety pin will fix the problem, I'm sure. And I bargained a very confused Leila down to a buck and a quarter for a Red Wings (men's large) jersey. She threw in a pair of high-top crew socks and didn't ask me any questions. I love her.

3 days
14 hours
15 minutes

I pull into the gated community. A guard sits in the booth but, no, he's not wearing a fuzzy black hat and red coat. He wears a turban with the name JOSE embroidered on the pocket of his jacket. I guess he had to borrow a shirt this morning.

"Can I please see your identification?" he asks in a thick Middle Eastern accent.

"Sure." I pull out my driver's license. "Are you the bouncer? Because I'm not eighteen yet, but will be in a few days."

He doesn't laugh—just checks my name off a list.

"Go ahead." He hands me back my license, and an iron gate lifts up and over my car like a guillotine.

I drive on cobblestoned streets—my car bounces along, testing the shock absorbers, probably blowing them out—and spot the address. I park behind my mom's car on the street and check out the gargantuan house in front of me. *Holy crap. I'm at the Disneyland castle.*

I cross the street, hear a whirring, and look up to see a camera turning, following every step I take. I wave, thinking maybe Principal Nathanson got himself a weekend job, and approach a stone gate. A five-by-five-inch plastic panel with a dozen buttons is nestled within one of the stones. *Which one do I hit?* I randomly push something and jump back as the first four chords of Beethoven's Fifth bellow, shouting to the neighbors, *Class. Do you hear that? It's called class.*

"Yes?" A voice from the stones.

"Uh, hi. I'm Beatrice Washington. I'm here to help . . ."

The buzzer buzzes, and the twenty-foot-tall wrought-iron gates part, revealing a castle complete with turrets. I wonder if there's a moat, and if so, where the bridge is and if there are trolls to watch out for.

The front door slowly opens as I make my way up the slate stone drive. A black woman, in (are you kidding me?) a friggin' white uniform and a white hat, stands at the door.

I thought slavery was abolished? "Hi." I offer my hand.

She hesitantly takes my hand. "Please, come in, Miss Washington."

"Bea. You can call me Bea. And yours?"

She looks down at her feet. "Martha," she mumbles.

"Martha. That's a beautiful name. Very nice to meet you. This is . . . quite some place you have here."

She giggles. "Oh, it's not mine, but thank you. I try to keep it up nice and all."

"Well, you do a great job. I think my mom is expecting me?"

"Yes, yes, of course. Follow me."

I take in the tacky, crystal-chandeliered foyer the size of a movie theater lobby. My voice echoes off the painted faux-marble walls.

She walks me up a sleek stairway with a mahogany banister. The carpet runner is hunter green with little flecks of gold. My UGG boots feel rather clunky as I climb the stairs, flattening the pile of the rug.

"Brrr . . . it's cold in here." I shiver. "I should have worn my robe over my pj's."

I think I hear a little laugh. "The temperature is set at sixty-eight degrees. It's best for the art, you see." She sounds like a robot, programmed by her master.

I check out the "art" that lines the walls. Phony expressionistic landscapes, pseudo modern minimalist (meaning empty) canvases lit by tiny spotlights. Art that you know was selected by a lame designer saying how *very* important it is. "I think you can raise the temp a couple degrees—in fact, turn it all the way up . . . burn it. Most of this stuff is crap."

And then I stop short in my boots. Because a friggin' Rembrandt etching hangs at the top of the stairs, tucked in a corner on the landing. No light illuminating it, it stands alone, crooked on the wall. I straighten it, "Do you know what this is, Martha? Who did this?"

"No. It's none of my business."

"Well, it should be. You are in the presence of a Rembrandt. I mean, if it's real. They obviously don't know what they have.

You know," I whisper, "you should, now and then, mention that you happen to like that picture—don't call it an etching, you'll give it away—of the old man's face at the top of the stairs." I tap the corner, making it crooked again. "You never know, you might get it for Christmas this year—instead of a bonus."

She covers her mouth like she just burped. "You think it's worth some money?"

"All I have to say is, if they give it to you? There's no more wearing a uniform for you. You'd be set for life."

Martha gasps, and then opens the door to a VERY PINK ROOM.

"Whoa." I shield my eyes. "Anyone have sunglasses?"

"Bea, there you are."

"I hear you but can't see you. Is that you, Mom?"

She ignores my antics. "Alanna, this is my daughter, Bea."

A blond, blue-eyed, perfect-looking little girl says nothing. She wears a short pink skirt—what a surprise—with a matching camisole with iridescent sequins on the straps. No boobs to speak of yet, but I bet it'll be on next year's birthday list. She looks me up and down—obviously not approving of my "look," her face sours. And then she texts something (for sure a diss) into her phone.

God, I know these girls. There were so many of them just like her at Athena Day School for Girls. Every single one with attitude as their middle name.

I eye her ginormous room. The bed could sleep a family of six, and there's enough down in the quilts and pillows to help a gaggle of Canadian geese fly to Florida, round trip—surrounded by what looks like a mosquito net. It makes me wonder if she's afraid of malaria.

"Alanna was telling me where she'd like the mural—we've been mapping it out." My mom points to pencil drawings etched on the wall.

"Anyway . . ." Alanna floats her right arm in the air and points. "I was thinking over there we'd draw Alice." She punctuates this with a smug smile.

"Oh, I like that idea. Now let's talk about the background. Do you have any thoughts on color?" Mom asks.

Let's see, I'm guessing she'll say . . .

"Pink!" Alanna shouts. Her smartphone *pings*. She reads, giggles, and types, and then sashays to the designated wall. "So, anyway, I was thinking of the Cheshire cat right here, sitting by Alice." She waves her hand. "The tea party over there, and oh, like, mushrooms growing up from the ground, and . . ."

I crack up.

The princess blinks her long lashes. "What's so funny?"

"You want 'shrooms on your wall?"

"Yeah, like in *Alice in Wonderland*."

"Oh, those kind." I nod. "But you do realize that Lewis Carroll was . . ."

An elbow shot from Mom, meaning, *bite your tongue, Bea.*

So I finish it in my head: *totally high on mushrooms when he wrote it?*

"Beatrice, why don't you get the drop cloth from out of my

car?" Mom asks, handing me her keys. She bends down in her low-rise jeans and starts unpacking paint materials.

"Sure. You got it." *Please, get me out of here before I say something I'll regret.*

As I pass Little Miss Muffet, she flips her hair and literally raises her nose in the air.

And I walk out the door, thinking, *maybe that's who Mom would really like for a daughter. She wouldn't complain about her hair—no way.*

I stop at the Rembrandt and cop another touch, think about pocketing it, but head down the stairs instead and open the front door. A series of chimes beep the words *open door, open door.*

Oh, hell. Now what did I do? I close the door—same thing, but *closed door, closed door* this time.

"It's the monitoring system." Martha peeks around the corner—her hat is off, her collar unbuttoned.

"Whew. I didn't break anything, right?"

"You really think that's a Rembrandt?" She glances up the stairs.

"Yup. Christmas, remember, plant the seed now." I walk outside and stand at the closed gate. Now what? Do I climb? Yell to Martha? I search for a button—something that says *get me outta here*, when the gates suddenly start to part. And I wonder for a second if my superhero power has suddenly morphed into telekinesis.

I jump out of the way of the moving gate and stand near a blooming hedge. The sickeningly sweet smell makes me sneeze, and the hedge is covered with buzzing bees—killer bees, I'm sure. A white Range Rover charges in—the driver, totally spaced, almost hits me.

"Hey, watch where you're going!" I scoot out of the gates before they close, cross the street to my mom's car, and unlock the trunk, thinking, *that's just like the white SUV that almost hit me in front of my house the other day.*

A short guy wearing a white sports ensemble, with a tennis racket under his arm, steps out of the truck. *Oh my god. Was he at my house with my mom that morning?*

He scratches his seventies-style thick, black moustache and waves, calls out, "Hello! You must be Beatrice. Bella's daughter."

I thought they weren't on a first name basis . . . wanted to keep it professional.

I pull the drop cloth out of the car and walk back up the drive.

He holds out his hand. "I'm Alanna's Dad, Michael."

I don't take it. "Uh-huh."

He pockets his hand in his tight white shorts.

I squint, stare at the 'stache. His hair is gray. There's no way he should have a black moustache. I suddenly get the urge to pull it off his face . . . see if it's fake.

His right eye twitches. "Um, is there something wrong?"

I don't know. Why don't you ask my dad?

"Well . . . okay, I guess I'll be going inside. Nice to meet you." He turns toward the front door.

Ugh! Just the thought of them together really burns me. "Are you messing around with my mom?" I call out.

He spins around—shifts his sneakered feet. "Excuse me?"

"Save the shit. You heard me."

"I don't know what you're talking about."

"Yeah, right, blah, blah, blah . . ."

"Really, you're confused, I assure you."

I take a step toward him. "All I have to say are two words: my dad. He's twice the size of you and a total badass."

Michael Dickwad Connelly nervously tee-hees. "I have no idea what you are talking about. I have no intentions—no relationship with your mother other than professionally. I hired her to design my little girl's mural."

"Oh, right. Your little girl, Alanna. If I were you, I'd get her off that pedestal. Knock it out from under her feet, fast. She's already deluded, living in a"—I point at the tacky house—"a fairy-tale world. She's gonna be using, flat-on-her-ass stoned, sexting, snapchatting before you know it—if she isn't already. I've seen it happen to a dozen Alanna's just like her."

"I beg your pardon . . ."

"You can beg all you want, but you're not pardoned—far from it."

His whole body posture changes, like he's an attack dog; his stance widens, his chin juts. "Who do you think you are, talking to me that way?"

"Someone who's been there, done that. And it ain't fun. Believe me." I'm on a roll, and can't stop—don't want to stop. "First off? Tell Martha to ditch the uniform. Alanna's watching you, seeing how you treat women—and you obviously don't think too highly of them. Second? Lock your liquor cabinet—everything, including wine and beer. Oh, yeah, throw in the sleep meds, the pot—whatever else is your drug of choice. Kids will try anything for a high. Third? Keep your wallet and checkbook on you at all times—any extra cash, stash it in a safe along with all the passwords to your accounts. Fourth? Don't believe a word she says from now until she's eighteen—hopefully she'll still be alive."

I think he's stopped breathing because his face has turned whiter than his sneakers, and a blue vein suddenly pops out of his right temple—blood pulsing. "Get out of here, now. Get off my property," he says through his clenched jaw.

"Sure. Happy to. Thought you'd never ask." I shove the drop cloth in his arms, dirtying up his tennis whites. "Give this to my mom, *Mrs.* Washington. You can tell her I was stung by a nasty wasp in the driveway and had a sudden allergy attack."

3 days
9 hours
30 minutes

ot, hot water rushes over my sore muscles, my blistered feet, my twisted hair, and drowns my tears.

Why? Why would she even think of doing this to us? She doesn't love us anymore? I'm not good enough? Dad's not good enough? What did we do? What did I do wrong?

I squeeze a dollop of conditioner on my hand, desperately trying to untwist Eva Marie's handiwork and soften the tangles. It hurts, pulls at my scalp. But the pain isn't as bad as what I feel in my heart, in the pit of my stomach.

My hair always got tangled and gnarly if I wore it down when I was a little girl, so Mom would braid it after my nighttime bath—it became a ritual. A ritual I loved, even if it hurt. I'd get to choose any book I wanted, and then my dad would come in and plop down, and the three of us would sit on my bed. Dad would read as my mom carefully combed through the tangles. Sometimes tears would form as she pulled, when

SNITCH

the comb got caught in a knot, but I kept them in, hid them in a secret place—a jeweled chest of tears, I imagined. I tried really hard to stop them from dripping down my face, because I didn't want her to stop combing. I didn't want my dad to stop reading. I didn't want to break our triangle of three, connected, sitting on my bed.

How could she do it? Dismantle the triangle?

I practically use the whole bottle of conditioner, most of the hot water, and finally the knots untie. I smooth my fingers through the tamed curls, and then use a wide-tooth comb, just like Mom did. I step out of the shower, wipe off the steamy mirror, and study myself, my reflection, my hair—wet, pulled down, stretched, and tucked behind my ears.

If only my hair could stay this way. For her. For me. For Dad. For the three of us.

3 days
4 hours
15 minutes

Thank god Wendell called, got me out of my pity party and asked me out. I'm thrilled to get out of the house. I don't want to face my mom—not yet, not with all the confusion flying around my brain. I blow away this morning's events with the hair dryer and fluff the life back into my cotton-candy look, smelling like coconut cream conditioner.

I slip on a short linen shift dress in raw sienna. It kind of has a twenties swing to it—even has the fringe on the bottom of the hem tickling my knees. I pair it with my desert-sand suede ankle boots and my jean jacket. It feels good to be tapping into the estrogen side of me.

It's a breezy night, in between storms. The pollen has been washed out of the air, curbing my sneezing and runny nose for the time being. I take a deep breath in and the clean, fresh air fills my lungs. Maybe I can quit smoking for good. Maybe that meanie Credos will scare the urge out of me.

We meet up at a Rosie's Café outside of Kerrytown—our usual place. It's one of those cute, warm-and-fuzzy, cottagey coffeehouses. Wannabe poets, singers, and musicians perform on a wooden platform in the corner of the room, which acts as a stage. Wendell and I love making fun of them afterward. I mean, not like we're criticizing the artists; it's just that we've never heard anything amazingly inspiring, and I'm always kind of embarrassed for them, sweating under the spotlight.

"This is nice." I hold his hand, happy to have a distraction, happy to be with someone who wants to be with me, crazy hair and all.

"It is. It's always nice with you."

"Awww." I kiss him on the cheek. "Thank you."

Wendell chooses a round, chunky table right in front of the stage.

I tug his shirt. "You sure you want to be so close to the stage? I mean, you never know who's going to perform. It could be a juggling act, and I don't think we want to get hit by any balls." I wait for his laugh. It doesn't come.

Wendell sits. *Okay, then, I guess this is it.*

We place our order with a bitchy waiter named Brad. It's his shtick, being a bitch, and doesn't really bother us. It's kind of comforting knowing what to expect with his sighs and attitude—mannerisms he wears as proudly as his Prada belt.

"Wen, you're quiet. You okay?" I pat his thigh.

"I'm fine, Bea." He smiles, and a blob of spittle forms in the corner of his mouth.

Brad sets down our cappuccinos in the middle of the table.

"You sure this is decaf?" Wendell asks him. "She's very sensitive to caffeine."

"Listen, lovely-ass, you think she's sensitive?" Brad hands him his card. "Call me if she's up in the middle of the night, and you're up because she's up; give me a buzz, and I'll shoot over with some sleepy-time tea. Oh, yeah, baby, I will. It's a special Brad brew." He arches a brow, fluffs the hair that isn't there, and walks away.

Wendell pulls two sugars from the little ceramic hollowed-out cat on the table, rips them open, pours them in my cup, and stirs.

"Are you going to hold the cup for me, too, Wendell?"

"I just want to make you happy."

Man, he's acting weird.

The lights dim. "Oh, great, must be talent-show time." I laugh.

Suddenly, Wendell clears his throat, stands, and steps toward the stage.

"Wen? What are you doing? What's going on?"

He takes a seat on a simple wooden chair in the middle of the dark stage. A microphone stand sits in front of him. A spotlight suddenly pops on and shines down, illuminating the dust in the air, casting an angelic halo over his head.

Oh, no. What's happening? What's he going to do?

Someone, from the darkness, hands him an acoustic guitar.

A guitar? He plays the guitar?

Wendell strums a few chords, tweaks the fret, clears his throat, starts to finger the guitar strings, and plays for a moment; and I relax a bit, because he's good. He sounds really good. *Whew.* I thought I'd have to pretend to like it. I sit back in my chair, hold my cup to my lips, and lick the frothy cinnamon foam.

Wendell taps the mike. "Test. Test." His low, scratchy voice amplifies in the room. "Um . . . I normally don't do this. Perform in front of people. But, ah, I have this very special person in my life right now. And it's almost her birthday."

Oh, no, please. . . . I put down my cup on the table.

"Anyway, I have no idea what to get her, because she has everything. She has everything a man would want in a woman. But the only thing this man is missing are answers to a few simple questions."

I want to bolt—out of this chair, out of the saccharine cuteness of the café, out of what I hope doesn't happen.

"Anyway, here goes. . . ."

And oh my god, a friggin' spotlight now shines on top of *my* head. I'm sure no one is seeing any halos—nothing angelic hovering above me, just dust.

"Bea, I have some questions, and I think the musician Jack Johnson, in his words, asks it best." He starts picking out the tune, singing the song "Questions."

I feel my hair drying up, on fire with the heat of the

spotlight. My mouth is dry, and I can't swallow. I sip at my coffee. It chokes going down, and I start coughing, drowning out the next couple lines, hoping to drown out all the words that he sings. I mime to Brad that I'm in dire need of some water. He whispers in my ear, "You're *so* not into him, right?"

"What?" I choke.

"Don't worry, doll, I won't say a word. Use 'em and abuse 'em, that's my motto. Your secret's safe with me."

Wen continues, smiling sweetly at me, repeating the words at the end of the song, "be untrue," a few times, and I want to stand and shout out, *Yes. I'm sorry I am untrue.* You figured me out. I'm a phony. Untrue to you. I'm sorry that you're up there singing that song so beautifully to someone who doesn't deserve it. Please, please point the spotlight at someone else. I noticed a girl in the back of the café when we came in. She looks like she would dig that song. Really dig you singing it to her. Love you kissing her and maybe doing more to her, more than what I'm giving you. I'm not good enough for you. . . . *I'm so sorry.*

The spotlight on the stage flicks off, and the audience madly applauds.

"Happy birthday, Beatrice Washington," he says into the mike, in the darkness.

Please don't say the words, please, please . . .

"I think I'm falling in love with you."

I put my face in my hands.

Wendell sets down the guitar, steps off the stage, and comes toward me. The audience's applause swells. He stands above me, holds out his hands for mine. I take them, and he pulls me into his warm chest, hugging me tightly. I hear his heart thumping—a heart that I'm not worthy of. He rocks me back and forth. And then he lifts my chin. His eyes are moist with tears—mine are bone dry. The only thing I'm feeling right now is guilt. Ugly, arid, desert-dry—the color of my boots—guilt. He ignores it and lightly kisses me on the lips. His mouth tastes like sand. I close my eyes. *I'm such a phony.* I rest my head on his chest and peer at the exit sign. The red glow, drawing me in, luring me toward it. I want to run to it, pray that it sucks me in and out the door.

This is so not fair to him.

Finally somebody, thankfully, turns the spotlight off me, off us, and I feel the cool breath of Wendell's whispering words. "Can you tell me, Bea? Answer my questions?"

"Um, that was lovely, Wendell, thank you."

I can see the disappointment; his thick lids close halfway, and his brow slightly wrinkles. His head tilts, like, *That's it? That's all you have to say?*

So I add, "Your coffee's getting cold." I sit at the table and try not to pay attention to the icy stares from the audience. Wendell joins me and immediately guzzles down his glass of water that Brad, being unusually thoughtful, somehow knew, sensed he needed. I watch Wendell's Adam's apple bob up and down as he swallows.

I wish I could love that Adam's apple. I do. The way he swallows. It's a nice-looking Adam's apple.

151

OLIVIA SAMMS

The café resumes its normal activity. Generic coffeeshop music flows through the speakers. The buzz of conversation starts up . . . and I feel like a dick.

Secrets and lies.

After a half an hour of awkward conversation, Wendell and I leave the café. I take a deep breath of the crisp night air and shiver. "Brrr. It's getting a little nippy."

He raises the collar on his jacket and stuffs his hands in his pockets.

I pull one of his hands out and wrap my fingers around it. It's the least I can do.

He smiles, weakly.

"That was so special, Wen. A wonderful present. Thank you."

"Sure."

He knows.

We turn the corner, heading out of Kerrytown, and walk hand in hand down the dimly lit side streets toward our parked cars.

A meter maid slowly makes her way up the road, checking every meter, waiting to pounce.

"Oh, shit. The meter. I forgot to feed it."

"Hell, so did I. I've got it, Bea. No worries." He lets go of my hand and starts to jog toward our cars.

Stop being so nice to me! I want to call out to him.

He stops suddenly, pats his pockets, and turns back to me. "Well, this is embarrassing. But I don't have any change."

"Here, take my purse. I think I have some quarters."

Wendell jogs up to me, I hand him my purse, and he dashes down the street.

I wave, yelling, "Hurry, Wen, she's stopping."

He runs faster down the street, clutching my bag.

Suddenly a cop car comes screeching up onto the curb in front of Wendell, cutting him off. Sergeant Daniels lunges out, tackling him and throwing him down to the concrete. "Let go of her purse now!" he orders.

Oh. My. God.

Wendell is facedown on the concrete. Daniels is on top of him. Wendell tosses my bag out in the middle of the road—splays his hands.

I run up to them. "What the hell are you doing? Get off him." I try to pry the sergeant off Wendell's back.

Daniels looks up at me. "But he took your . . . I thought he was . . ."

"Oh for chrissakes!" I throw my hands up in the air, circling, yelling at the gods. "This is my date, Wendell." I bend down. "Are you okay?"

"Oh," the sergeant says. And lifts his heavy body off Wendell's back.

"*Oh?* That's all you have to say?"

Wendell sits up, stunned, and keeps his scraped hands in the air.

"You can put your hands down; he's nobody important. Just Sergeant Dan Daniels, from the Ann Arbor Police. He's harmless."

Wendell, always polite, awkwardly reaches out his hand to shake. His palms are scratched, bleeding a bit. "Um, nice to meet you, ah . . . sir . . . Sergeant."

Daniels embarrassingly accepts his hand and hoists Wendell up, back on his feet. "You okay? I didn't hurt you, did I?"

Wendell brushes off his pants, spits on his scraped hands. "I think I'm all right. A little shook up, but okay, I guess."

I shake my head in disbelief. "This is unreal. What were you thinking, Daniels? And why the hell were you . . ." I look around at the near-empty street. "Are you following me again?"

"No. I happened to be driving by. I thought he was . . ."

"I know what you thought. You thought Wen, who happens to be black, was mugging me. Jesus Christ. You were profiling."

"I was not profiling."

"Bea, I don't think that's what it was," Wendell interjects. "He was just doing his job."

"No, he was profiling." I turn to the sergeant. "What if he were white, huh? Would you have jumped him then?"

"Bea . . . it's okay, really."

I shush Wendell with my hand. "It's not okay. Stay out of my life, Dan!"

"Hey. You've gotten yourself in some dangerous situations. How was I supposed to know you were out on a date? You've never mentioned you were dating anyone."

"What? Are you kidding me? Why would I do that? Are you going to have a problem with every guy I go out with? Beat them up? Throw them out of town?"

"Every guy?" Wendell asks.

"Marcus was a loser. You know that," Daniels says.

"Marcus? You're seeing other people?" Wendell takes a step back.

"No, Wen. I'm not seeing anyone else. I just meant that I don't need his protection."

Daniels walks into the street, bends, picking up my purse. I march over to him. "Give me that! I am not a damsel in distress, and I don't need your help." I snatch it out of his hands.

"I know that, Bea, but I think you think you're tougher than you really are."

"Bull. I am tough."

"Not as tough as those gang kids, not even close."

"Oh, Christ. You *have* been following me."

"Cole saw you. At the track. Said he saw the tagger punk that I brought in the other day at the station."

"God, he's such a tattletale."

"You're pretending to be a boy with that team? Are you nuts?"

"I didn't pretend anything. The coach assumed it."

"How did you know about that gang, anyway?"

"Gang? Pretending to be a boy? Bea, what is he talking about?" Wendell's looking royally confused.

"Nothing. He's confusing me with someone else."

Daniels blows through his lips, lowers his voice. "What are you not saying? You know something—how else would you have found them?"

I break eye contact.

"Stay away from them, Bea—you hear me? It's not safe. Leave the case to me."

"And why would I do that? What are you doing about it, huh?"

"We're narrowing in on a suspect."

"Well, narrowing isn't fast enough. Someone shot that Junior kid in the head. Who's going to be next?"

"Hopefully not you!" he yells. "Dammit! You shouldn't be hanging out with gangs."

"I'm not. . . . It's a friggin' track team. They give food to the homeless for chrissakes. And Wendell, look at him, he's not in a gang. . . . Jesus!" I stamp my boot.

"I know, I know . . . I said I was sorry." Daniels turns. "You're okay, right?"

We search for Wendell.

"Wen? Wendell, where d'you go?"

He's halfway down the street, shoulders slumped. Doesn't even bother to face us. Keeps heading toward his car. "I'm going home, Bea," he calls out. "I know when I'm not wanted."

"Wendell, no. Please, stay."

He waves his hand, shooing us away. "You two apparently have some unfinished business to work out, and I don't want to be in the middle. Thanks for tonight. Oh, and by the way. . . ." He stops, faces me. "You answered my questions. Have a good birthday."

Beep, beep, beep. The car chirps as he unlocks it with his remote, hops in, starts the engine, and rolls off into the darkness.

"Dammit! Now look what you did." I kick an old bottle top into the gutter. "Can't you just mind your own business?"

"I said I'm sorry."

"I could've grown to like him . . . I think . . . maybe."

"Well, why would this stop you—the two of you? Go after him, Bea. Go on."

"Ughhh . . . ," I growl. "You don't get it, do you?"

"What? What don't I get?"

"Wendell just said it. The unfinished business, you fool." I twirl, stomping in the middle of the street like a two-year-old having a temper tantrum. "Shit, shit, shit. You!"

"You mean an old fart like me could actually compete with a stud like that?"

"No. You can't," I say unconvincingly.

And then, like two opposite-pole magnets, we are pulled together in the middle of the street—have no control, can't resist, and don't want to. We take baby steps toward each other—inches apart and then . . . stop.

Our hands are at our sides, frozen. And yet his green eyes dissolve into my hazel ones. The colors pool around, and I'm suddenly filled with all the answers. Flooded. The only answer I know—the only constant in my life is him, Sergeant Dan Daniels. There are no questions. None.

And in my head—without a pen in hand, a sheet of paper, we are there—in each other's arms. I can feel him kiss my neck. My arm reaches up, and I touch the downy fluff at his nape, smell the smell that was meant for me, only for me, that takes me to where I belong, where I need to go. Grounds me. No questions. My hand runs through his blond hair, and he cradles me against his chest. I hear the heart I am supposed to be hearing—the steady beat—in sync with mine. And he lifts my chin, and our lips touch, ever so softly. I let myself fall into the deliciousness of his taste, like nothing I've ever tasted before, and it is *right*. So right, so safe. All my senses are engaged, alive . . . and imagined.

"Everything okay, Sarge?" A fellow cop in a passing car calls out the window.

Sergeant Daniels takes a step back from me. Addresses his colleague. "Yeah, everything's fine. Why?"

"Just that you were in the middle of the street, frozen-like. She okay?" He points at me.

"Yeah." He nods. "She's okay. We're okay."

"See you at the station." He drives off.

Daniels reaches into his car. Hands me my Moleskine. "Here. You dropped this. Thought you may be missing it."

"Thanks."

He places his hand lightly on my back. "Let me walk you to your car."

We're quiet for a few steps.

"I'm twenty-eight," he says.

"Big whoop. I'm almost eighteen."

"And I'm a cop."

"Yeah, well, that's the weird part for me. You being a cop—not how old you are." We get to my car. A ticket's stuffed under the windshield wiper. "Oh, man. For real?"

He grabs it, shoves it in his back pocket. "I'll take care of it."

"Guess that's one good thing about knowing you."

"You're welcome."

"Thank you."

We stand there awkwardly.

"What are you doing for your birthday?" he finally asks.

"Not much. Dinner with my folks."

"After that?"

"I don't know. Will you be following me?"

"Perhaps."

"So, I'll see you then, right?"

"Yeah." He smiles, leans down, and then whispers in my ear. "But don't dress like a boy, okay?"

I melt.

3 days
45 minutes

I tiptoe into my dark house, tiptoe into the unknown, and pray I don't wake the parents. I don't want to see Mom. I'm afraid to see her. She has to be over-the-top pissed because . . .

A. Mr. Michael Connelly, moustache guy, told her everything I said to him, and she lost her job.
B. She shared with Dad, in which case he's probably over-the-top pissed, too.
C. She confessed to Dad about her affair, in which case he's heartbroken, and how the fuck am I going to deal with that?
D. All of the above.

I've always hated multiple choice. I'm screwed no matter what the answer is.

Their bedroom door opens. "I'll talk to her," I hear Dad say.

The landing at the top of the stairs creaks, the door squeaks closed, and then his heavy, measured footsteps make their way downstairs.

I decide to tough it out on the couch in the living room—an odd name for the room, because no one is ever in here, no one lives in it, not even close. It's like a distant cousin once removed or something—a part of our house, but not really.

Dad enters the dark room and switches on a table lamp—the base a glazed clay sculpture of my mom's—the figure of a nude woman, beautiful, like a Matisse, I've always thought. She told me she made it in college freshman year and that my dad wired and converted it into a lamp as a surprise birthday present a year later. She hated that he did that. Thought he ruined it, and, yeah, I think he did, too. So it's in a room that nobody's ever in. All alone. I'm surprised it hasn't accidently-on-purpose been knocked over and broken with the infrequent dustings.

My dad sits on the couch next to me. Says nothing.

"Is Mom okay?" I stupidly ask.

"What do you think?"

I shrug my shoulders.

"She lost her job, Bea. So, no, she's not okay."

Oh, crap, the answer is A. But then again, why am I surprised? *Did she lose her lover, too?*

His large, dark hands touch his mouth as if he's praying. He speaks through tented fingers. "Why did you do it, Bea? What made you say those things?"

Circle B, too.

"You hurt that little girl's feelings, Bea."

"What? I what?"

"Not everyone is used to your sarcastic humor and a personality as strong as yours. She's only ten."

"That's why Mom was fired? But I barely spoke to the girl, Dad." *I certainly didn't say as much as I wanted to.* I sink back into the couch cushion. *Oh my god; he's clueless. He has no idea. Answer C is out of the running. Mom didn't fess up.*

"I'm sure there will be other jobs, but this was a big one." He fingers the tweed piping of the couch. "You owe a huge apology to your mother, you know that, right? And now she's not sure that having you as her assistant this summer is going to work out. Is that why you did it, Bea? I know you don't want to work with her. Did you sabotage this on purpose?"

I wish it were that simple. "No, of course not."

"She's taking a hot bath now, calming down, and is thinking of driving to Chicago tomorrow, to visit her parents."

I sit forward. "Gramma and Grandpa?" I think I've only met them once, maybe twice. I don't even remember what they look like, I was so little. But I get a card from them every Christmas and every birthday—signed *with love, Gramma and Grandpa*—as if everything were normal. "Mom hasn't spoken to them in years. Why now, Dad?"

"I think it's all about turning forty. She reached out to them, and they to her."

"When is she coming back?"

"I don't know." He takes his glasses off and rubs the bridge of his nose. "I just don't know."

Is she leaving us? Leaving my dad?

I stand, and kiss *him* on the top of the head. "It'll be okay, Dad," I try to convince him . . . and myself. "We'll be okay."

1 day
11 hours
45 minutes

I sit on the hood of my car in the school parking lot. "I have a question for you."

"Shoot." Billy balances on his skateboard, rolls himself a smoke—tobacco this time.

"You're so friggin' smart."

"Not a question." His eyes crinkle as he lights.

"Why'd you do it?"

"What? Why'd I do what?" He offers me a hit.

I wave it away. "Take the SAT for Zac?"

"Hah. Oh, that." He spits a bit of tobacco in the air. "You said it. 'Cause I'm friggin' smart." He smiles a shit-ass grin at me.

I tuck my knees into my chest. "You actually took the test for him? Wow."

"How'd you find out, little Miss Killa Bea?"

"Oh, come on, the guy's an oaf."

SNITCH

"You got that right; the dude's a no-brainer, but no way he'd cop to it. He's scared as shit someone will suss him out. How d'you know?"

"Someone brought up your name in the lunchroom, said something like, *even Billy Weisman couldn't have scored that high* and Zac shut up—got squirmy wormy when your name was mentioned. I sort of guessed you had something to do with it, but I thought you'd deny it."

"Who said I couldn't score that high?"

I laugh, jump off the hood. "How did you two get away with it?"

"Cinch. It's like a scene, man. Mobbed. Took it up in Pontiac. Damn. Don't know if the proctors can't read, or if they didn't care. And without the goat?"—he pulls at his chin patch—"I be Mr. Zac's doppelgänger, no?" He flicks the cigarette off into a puddle on the asphalt. It sizzles to its death.

"Not even close, Billy; you don't look anything like him."

"Whatever." He kicks the backside of the board and it seesaws, shoots straight up in the air like a yo-yo, and lands gracefully in his arms.

"You still haven't answered my question. Why did you do it?"

"*Beaucoup* bucks." He rubs his fingers together. "I scored a couple grand—rent check—saved my pop's shop."

"Got it." I nod. "But you could be arrested. Zac could get kicked out of Cornell. You know that, right?"

"Only if someone rats." He drops the board, jumps on again. "And you wouldn't do that, right?"

165

"Nah. But it kills me knowing he's a fraud. He's such a dick."

"Keep it on the sly. You chill?"

"I'm chill."

He kick-starts on his board and rolls off.

Chris comes running up. "There you are. . . . I was looking all over for you."

"Oh, sorry. I had some business with Billy to take care of."

"Business? What kind of business?"

"It's nothing." We head toward school.

Chris's eyes narrow. "Why are you hanging out with him?"

"Because I like him?"

Chris takes my arm, stops me. "Bea . . . tell me the truth, are you using? I saw him smoking a joint."

"That wasn't weed. It was a cigarette. And even if it were a joint, I wouldn't have had any. Jesus, doesn't anyone in this world trust me?"

"I don't want anything to happen to you. I don't want you to fall back into . . . bad habits."

"Will you please lay off of that, Chris?" I open the school doors, and walk fast to my locker.

"Bea. I'm dead serious." Chris follows. "You've been acting all twitchy, dressing different. I saw you leaving school the other day in your baggy jeans, and that awful red hoodie of mine—you wouldn't be caught dead in them normally."

"I wear the jeans when I'm on the rag, okay? Feeling a little water-weight gain."

"I'm not stupid. These are all the signs. And Billy—he's not exactly who you should be hangin' with."

"God, you sound like my mom. No. I'm not doing drugs, Chris. And Billy? He happens to be really cool when you get to know him. Yeah, he's not going to college, doing what he *should* do, according to you, according to most of the kids in this hellhole school. It doesn't mean he's stupid. He happens to be the smartest person I ever met, okay? Probably will be more successful than any college frat boy. And guess what? He actually was interested in *my* plans—he took the time to look at my sketchbook, my tattoo designs . . ."

Chris's face flushes; a pinkish-red hue starts at his cheekbones, travels to his jaw, and creeps down covering his neck. "This isn't about Billy anymore, is it?"

I slam my locker shut. "Look, Chris, I'm sorry I said all that. I didn't mean it. The last couple of days have been crazy." I lean my forehead against the cold metal door and lower my voice. "I drew the truth out of Zac, and found out that Billy took the test, the SAT for him. Okay? That's what this is all about. You happy now?"

He takes a huge intake of breath. "Holy shit, no."

"Holy shit, yes." And then I totally regret telling him. "Oh my god, you cannot, I repeat, sooo cannot tell anyone, okay, promise me?"

Chris is doubled over, laughing his ass off. "What a loser. He thinks he's such hot shit. This is priceless! He's a fucking fraud."

"Shhhh! Chris, promise me!"

"I promise." He wipes a tear. "But it . . . it's, like, whoa. Wouldn't it be great to get on Nathanson's loud speaker and expose the ass?"

"Stop it!"

"Can I tell Ian?"

"No."

I take his hands in mine. "Look at me." He does; his nostrils flare with suppressed laughter. "It's going to kill you, going to be hard knowing he's getting away with it. But we've got to let it go. . . . Sometimes, a lot of the time, knowing the truth sucks."

$$1 \ day$$
$$8 \ hours$$
$$26 \ minutes$$

I hurry home and bandage my heel with cotton balls and Scotch tape (the only tape I can find), lay out today's outfit on my bed (thanks to Leila), and pull on the pair of shin-high crew socks. I haven't shaved my legs in days. I'm not as hairy as most boys, but definitely more than Chris and Mohawk Johnny, and with the long, shiny nylon workout shorts (the safety pin helped with the waist issue), the bottom half of me, I think, works.

I flatten my boobs with a sports bra and pull on the baggy Red Wings jersey. But it's threatening to rain again today and only in the fifties, so the hoodie should be cool with the coach.

And now my dreaded hair.

I have to flatten the fluff. . . . It's time for gel. I dip my fingers into the cold, slimy goo and spread it liberally through my hair, slicking it back. Then I aim the dryer and blow it dry. By the time I've finished, it's like I'm wearing a helmet—it's as

169

hard as a shell on a turtle's back. I knock on it, and the noise echoes in my ears.

I crunch the baseball cap on top of my head, backward this time, take a deep breath, and peek in the mirror. I haven't waxed the 'stache for a good week, and with my hair back I actually have sideburns (Mom's genes). And my hair sticks out from under the hat all frizzy-like (Dad's genes). Not a good look—almost makes me want to cry—but I suck it up like a man, ready to take on today's events.

Someone *has* to know something about what happened to Junior. I have to crack the case. . . . I have to. I owe it to him.

• • •

Click. The stopwatch starts, and I run. My muscles are still cranky but not screaming, which is a good thing, and my legs are a little lighter, bouncier with real sneakers on my feet. I make it around the corner without dying, and there's no black gook coming up from my lungs, at least not yet.

Click. I lean my hands on my knees, breathing hard. "How'd I do, Coach?"

"You suck." He slaps me on the back, almost knocking me over.

"But I was better, faster, right? I made it around this time."

"Don't ask for praise from me, Boy. Do it for yourself. You're the only one that counts, not me. Give me fifty crunches. Now."

Shit. I fall to the wet ground, knowing there's no use arguing with him, and start the sit-ups, cursing him with every breath.

Archie comes running up to me, holds my feet. "Hey, B."

"Hey, Arch." A little awkward, my position on the ground with him at my feet, but I continue crunching up like any dude would.

"Your piss musta been clean, huh?"

I grunt and nod.

"Yeah, I never touch the stuff." He points to his head. "Wanna keep this temple pristine, clear, focused." He gestures for a fist bump—I give him one, and he bumps me so hard the pain shoots up my arm.

He leans in and whispers, "Hey. You said you tag a little?"

"Shut up." I look around to see where the coach is. "You want him to add another fifty?"

"Nah. I thought maybe you'd wanna hang out, do some art. Johnny and I were thinking of hitting the Tridge tomorrow."

"In Ypsilanti?"

"Yeah."

"But the coach . . . that's one of his beefs, taggin'."

"It's my art, man." He thumps his chest. "He can't stop that, and he doesn't have to know, right?"

My belly's on fire as I grunt the words. "Yeah, right."

"So you in?"

"I dunno."

"Forget it." He stands. "It was our *thing*. Me, Johnny, and Junior. We were the three musketeers."

I reach the fiftieth sit-up and collapse on my side; searing pain rips through my abs. "Okay. Let me think about it." *He had me at* Junior.

Reyna and her sidekick, Roxanne, walk by and flip me the bird.

"Hell, they hate me," I say to Arch.

"No, they don't. They got their mojo goin' on. It's what they do. Act tough and all that. Have to spray their scent on new predators."

Speaking of predators, what sounds like a very angry lion roaring echoes across the field. The coach stands, towers over Johnny, poking his stubby fingers hard into his skinny chest. Johnny appears to be crying. "Get your ass in my office, now."

"Talk about tough; he's a monster," I say to Archie.

"Yeah, well, it looks like Johnny screwed up. He already has a couple strikes against him. Major pothead—can't get off the weed."

Johnny blubbers, "I'm sorry, Coach. I'm sorry." And then he scuffles toward the gym.

"What will the coach do if he catches us tagging?"

"Probably kill us." He snorts.

That's not even close to being funny.

Coach Credos starts in on us. "What you doin', huh? Getting your beauty rest? Start moving. Everybody, a two hundred. Every twenty feet backward. Now!" He charges toward the gym, following Johnny.

I begin the run and immediately launch into a coughing fit.

I spit to the side, and the goober almost hits Reyna, coming up from behind me. She elbows me in the stitch of my ribs super hard, and I stumble, wipe out, skidding on the wet, slick rubber . . . big time. Half of my knee skin lies on the track. Blood everywhere.

Archie jogs over to me, bends down. "Oh, man. That's nasty. You gotta get it bandaged. Go see the coach—he'll patch it up."

Reyna stands over me, checking out her manicure. "Nasty, that's for sure, mmm-hmm."

"Why'd you do that, Reyna?" Archie yells at her.

"Boy knows why, don't cha bitch?" She sniggers, taking Roxanne's hand in hers. They skip ahead.

I'm *so* not fooling the girls.

I don't want to see Credos, go back in the guy's locker room, but I know I have to, the way my knee is bleeding, and I limp over to the gym. I've never been good with blood. Never. It makes my tummy twitch like panicked worms in a tin can.

The basketball chicks are shooting baskets again as I limp to the guy's locker room, push open the door, and close my eyes. Thankfully, there aren't naked butts staring at me. (Okay, I peeked.) I hear the showers running and what I think is Johnny crying. I *really* don't want to see Johnny's long john, so I hobble to an office that's surrounded by glass reinforced with crosshatched wire.

Coach Credos stands with his back to me, and pulls his chair to the corner of the room. I hide behind a locker and watch him. He steps up on it and lifts one of the ceiling panels—pulls out a bottle of vodka, takes a long, deep swallow, puts it back, and then lowers the panel back in place. He steps off the chair and drags it back to his desk, sits, then runs his hands over his shiny bald orb.

Oh my god. The ceiling tile, that's it! What I thought was dimpled pumice stone was actually a ceiling tile. Pale gray, banded in metal strips. It's where he hides his shit—there's probably more . . . another hidden stash up there. *He's the OG—has to be! I have to get to Sergeant Daniels and let him know.* I do an about-face, ready to limp away.

"What's your problem, Boy?" he yells from his office. "How long have you been standing there?"

"Oh, um . . . I just got here now, and it's nothing much. I fell on the track, and my knee. It's bleeding a little."

He gruffly waves me in. "Sit down."

I do, and he checks out the oozing wound. "That's not a little." He takes out a first aid kit from the closet, rolls my sock down, and wipes the blood off with a piece of gauze. It catches on the grown-out stubble on my leg. The coach looks up at me—he for sure knows I shave. "I haven't had time to look over your paperwork, Boy . . ."

Good. Because I never turned it in.

"Tell me, how d'you find out about us?"

I sit a little straighter. "Junior told me."

"What?" His boozy breath spittles a little in my face. "Junior?"

"Yeah. Do you know how he's doing?"

"So, you heard what happened."

I nod.

"Touch and go, they say. How did you know him?"

"You mean how *do* I know him?" I challenge.

"Of course, of course that's what I meant."

"Through a friend," I lie. "I sure hope they catch whoever shot him." I stare directly in his eyes. "Lock him up for life."

Credos looks down, tends to my knee. He dabs the wound with what feels like battery acid. It burns like hell and I'm wondering if there'll be any kneecap left when I leave. But I'll probably never have to worry about shaving that part of my leg. No way. Every hair follicle depilated, now growing and blossoming on the track—a little patch of me. He then wraps it with gauze and tape, a tad tighter than I think is necessary.

I jump up and my leg almost gives out from under me, but I force it to take my weight. "Thanks, Coach," I say.

"No problem. You know, you should probably take it easy the next week—give it time to heal."

"Oh, okay, right."

"So, we'll see you in a week or so—no worries about coming here to practice." He sits at his desk, clearly dismissing me, clearly wanting me out his nonexistent hair.

The rain has started up again. I totter over to my car and see Reyna and Roxanne leaning up against it in the parking lot. "What you want, Boy? What's your story?" Reyna circles around me, checking me out, up and down, and blows a wolf whistle. "Ain't he sweet, Roxanne?"

Roxanne pinches my butt and makes a guttural purring noise.

I feel naked, exposed, degraded.

Reyna whispers, hisses in my ear. "You get into Archie's pants, bitch, I'll chop off your pretty little tits."

Gulp.

"Yeah, I know. You got the LBGT goin' on . . . but I don't give a fuck. He's mine. You got that?" She lifts her arm, and I instinctively cover my face, remembering Junior's words: *They go for your face* . . . and run to the other side of my car, listening to her cackle, jump in my Volvo, and peel out of the parking lot.

A black-and-white immediately pulls out behind me, and lights flash in my rearview mirror. *Oh, hell, this can't be happening.*

And wouldn't you know it? Friggin' Detective Cole, hitching up his pants, all full of himself, like he caught the big one of the day, walks up to my window. "License and registration."

"What did I do?"

"I said, license and registration."

I reach for my backpack on the seat next to me . . . it's not there. Look in the backseat. *Damn. I left it at the track.* I swallow calmly, say, "I think I left my wallet back at the school."

"You're driving without a license?"

"I said, I think it's back . . ." *No, wait. I don't want him to see my license. He'll know who I really am.* "Sorry, I don't have it."

He pulls out a pad from his back pocket. "I'm going to have to write you up."

I bite my tongue, wanting to scream, *You're not a fucking patrol officer.*

"Excuse me?"

Oh, shit. I guess I did scream it.

"Out of your car, now."

He frisks me . . . kind of pauses when he feels up my flattened breasts.

Third time I've been outed today. Damn.

• • •

I'm in the backseat. My handcuffed wrists (yet again) sit on my lap. "Driving without a license," he says. "Argumentative with a police officer," he tells someone (probably the sergeant) on his police walkie-talkie thing, which looks like a plastic toy, attached to his belt.

Weird, I think to myself (this time for sure to myself). *I've always been argumentative with the Sarge, and he's never arrested me. . . .*

"You're the punk that Sergeant Daniels brought in the other day, aren't you?"

I try to ignore his grating voice and stare out the passenger side window. I'm tempted to jump out of the car while on the freeway, but decide against it—only because it would give Detective Cole major pleasure to see me as roadkill splattered on the pavement.

"There's something up with you . . . something sketchy."

Sketchy. Hmmm . . . that gives me an idea. I wrestle my hands onto the waist of my shorts, squeeze the safety pin open—he didn't find that with the frisk; I think my bound breasts kind of distracted him a little—pull it out of the elastic, and grasp it in my right hand. I have absolutely no idea if this will work—have never tried it with a pin.

"What'd you say your name was?" I ask.

He adjusts his rearview mirror—peers at me with surprised eyes and doesn't answer.

I wriggle around in the seat belt, trying to get a better look at his eyes in the mirror. And then I notice bags of greasy fast-food wrappers on the floor at my feet.

"Stop squirming!" he orders.

"Oh, sorry. I'm just a little stressed—I'm sure you understand. You know, I've tried meditation, breathing exercises . . . it doesn't work for me. What do you do? I mean, your job, there must be a lot of anxiety and stress that goes along with it, right?"

"Keep quiet!" he barks.

"I'm just curious. How do you stay chill?"

"Mind your own business." He sneers at me in the mirror, and I get full-on eye contact . . . and suddenly images of food . . . ice-cream cones, cookies, potato chips, a gross amount of junk fill me up as I etch out a circle—a doughnut—in the pleather of the backseat.

"Isn't it great to have a couple Big Macs to keep you

company now and then . . . a nice, gooey glazed doughnut to hang with? Ahhh . . ."

He screeches into the station parking lot.

Sergeant Daniels is waiting—hurries up to the car. I guess it *was* the Sarge Cole was talking to.

"I got 'im." My door flings open, and Daniels yanks my arm. "Thanks, Cole. Thanks for picking him up."

As I'm pulled out of the car, I look back at the detective. He sucks in his pooched belly and lifts his double chin.

• • •

"It's Coach Credos. He's the kingpin. I know it."

I've moved from one vehicle to another, and now sit in the sergeant's parked car—in the front seat this time. It's kind of perfect that Cole dragged me here since I needed to give Daniels the latest info. The rain starts coming down hard now, pinging like bullets on the roof.

The Sarge unlocks the handcuffs. "I told you to leave it alone. Not to mess with that group. What the hell were you doing?"

"Working out?"

"And what happened to your knee?" He touches it.

I almost shoot through the roof. "Crap, that hurts. Why'd you touch it?"

"I told you this was dangerous, Bea. Why don't you ever listen to me?"

"I have something to tell you." I scoot around, look him squarely in his eyes. "I lied to you. Big time. You were right. Junior's innocent. He wanted to stay in jail because he knew exactly what would happen to him—he knew he'd be hurt. And it's all my fault."

"How did you know about the Kodiak Kidz?"

"The logo, the bear claw. I drew it out of him when I was in the cell and then googled it. It wasn't hard to find."

The windows start to fog. He switches on the ignition, cracks a window, and exhales. "I'm not happy about this. Not at all."

"I'm sorry. I really am. I thought if Junior stayed in jail, maybe he'd be safe, like he said. I had no idea you'd have to release him so soon."

"Do you get it? How much danger you're walking into? Most of those kids came from gangs . . . some violent gangs."

"I know, but that Coach Credos, he's the worst—a mean bastard." I shiver. "And I think he's the OG."

"Bea . . ."

"No, listen. I figured it out. I think he set Junior up to keep him quiet. Junior told me that he and the Jamal kid saw him with his stash. I did, too. This afternoon."

"What stash? We checked out Credos. We've been talking with him, and he's been cooperative, *very* cooperative, an inspiration for the community. The City Council voted him citizen of the year last year."

"Well, he's fooling everybody. He's hiding stuff in his office.

I saw it—with my own eyes. He always smells of booze—has vodka hidden above a ceiling tile in his office. He's living a lie, Sarge. You've got to trust me on this."

"Why? Tell me why I should trust you? You already lied to me once."

"I said I was sorry. Okay?"

"Oh, damn. Quick—duck!"

"What?"

He pushes me down on the floor in front of the seat—throws his jacket over me as I hear a knock on the window, and Detective Cole's voice.

"Hey, Sarge. What'd you do with that punk?"

"Letting him sit with it a while in a cell—stew, think it over."

And that's exactly what I'm doing, sitting with it, stewing, on the floor of his car.

"Good idea. There's something about him . . . doesn't sit right with me," Cole adds.

"Yeah, well, I think he learned his lesson this time."

"Man, it's raining hard. Why you out here, anyway?"

I hear rustling of a paper bag. "I thought I'd grab a bite."

"In the parking lot?" Cole asks.

"Why not?"

"Okay, whatever. I'm going to get a bucket of KFC; you want any?"

Of course he is.

"Nah. I'm cool."

I hear Cole walking away, whistling. Daniels pulls the jacket off me.

"How many years will I get if I kill him?" I ask, still on the floor.

"Bea. He's a good cop, works hard."

"Yeah, I know. You got the good cop, bad cop thing going on."

His phone *pings* with a text. He reads and then bites into his sandwich. Chews like his jaws have rusty hinges.

"You look weird."

"Thanks."

"No, I mean, your face. It looks stuck or something. Who texted you?"

"My ex. She's talking about moving out of town—with my son. She's engaged."

"Oh, man, I'm sorry." I sit back up on the seat. "Where to?"

"Chicago. She got a job in a law firm."

"Well, shoot, that isn't very far—just five hours or so."

"With my schedule? I'll be lucky if I see Max once a month—and weeknight visits—those will never happen. Do you know that last time I was there, picking him up? I actually heard him call the other guy *daddy*."

"Ouch. So what are you going to do?"

"I don't know yet, except enjoy every minute I have with him. I'm thinking of taking him to the new aquarium on Belle Isle this week, on my day off."

"This week?" I hold my breath.

He puts his hand on top of mine, like he's reading my mind. "Don't worry. I'll see you on your birthday."

"You mean follow me on my birthday." I work up a smile.

He takes his warm hand off mine and stuffs it in his pocket. And I find myself suddenly jealous of the damn pocket.

"I'd better get back to work—I do that, you know, work."

"I know, I know. It just seems to take so long to get anything done. You think you could give me a ride back to my car at Skyline?"

"Will you go straight home from there?"

I nod. "Are you going to check on the ceiling tile?"

"I will, if you promise me something."

"What?"

"That you'll never lie to me again. Promise?"

"I swear, never again."

"And no more track practice with those kids."

"Hell, no. I don't think I could run, anyway, the way my knee is." So, *maybe I'll tag instead.*

1 day
5 hours
45 minutes

don't see her car in the drive. I guess she's not home from Chicago yet. That means no explanation about what I'm wearing or the bloody bandaged knee. But more important, it means I won't have to deal with the wrath of Mom for making her lose her job—or more accurately, for the truth of *why* she lost her job.

I start up the stairs.

"Why did you do it, Bea?"

I peek around the corner and see her in the dining room, her back to me. She's wearing her overalls, standing on a chair, painting, covering the full wall—all the way up to the ceiling.

"Mom. I didn't know you were home. Where's your car?"

"In the shop. It needed an oil change after the long drive." Her right hand flings a swirl of angry black paint at a scary face—a mouth screaming, wide open, bloodshot eyes—a hand pulling at hair. Not exactly a children's mural. Far from it.

"How was Chicago?"

"Fine. Give me a cigarette."

"What?" I feel my face flush. "I quit."

"Bull. I saw a pack in your purse the other day."

"Okay," I fess up. "But I'm cutting back. They don't really help with my allergies." *Or my running.*

"So, give me one." She holds out her hand from behind her.

"But you don't smoke."

"I have been lately. Been lifting a few from your bag."

"Mom."

She snaps her fingers.

"Fine." I pull the pack out of my backpack and hand her one.

She steps off the chair, turns, and faces me. "I need a light."

I flick my Bic. She inhales. "I hope you do quit." She ironically exhales. "Your father and I hate that you picked up that habit back in rehab last year." She taps ash into a coffee mug and sits. "What are you wearing? And what happened to your knee?"

"I fell."

"Why did you do it, Beatrice?"

"What?" I play dumb. "Fall?"

"You know what I mean."

"You tell me what I know."

"Mr. Connelly told me what you said to him."

"You mean Michael?"

"It wasn't appropriate."

"Appropriate? Are you kidding me? Like you have the right to tell me what's appropriate, Mom?" I pull up a chair and sit across from her. Our eyes are level. "Do you still love Dad?"

She abruptly stands, facing the wall, dangling the cigarette in her mouth, and adds a bloodred flame shooting out of the snaggle-toothed monster.

"Why do you want to hurt him?"

"I don't."

"Then why?"

"Why what?" she growls, throwing her paintbrush down on the floor. I watch the red paint bleed into the beige carpet.

"Why are you cheating on him?"

She shakes her head. "You don't understand the whole situation, Bea."

"Explain it to me then." I stand. "I'm going to be eighteen . . . an adult. Stop babying me, okay?"

"I don't baby you."

"Yes, you do. You treat me like I'm handicapped. I messed up. I admit it. But I've been working like a dog to try and prove to you and Dad that I can stand on my own two feet."

She faces me, her eyes filled with tears. "You have, and I'm proud of you."

"Good, I'm glad you are, because after graduation I want to get an apartment and move out—live on my own."

"What?" She takes a step toward me. "No. No. We need each other. We only have each other."

"Uh-uh, Mom. *You* need me. You need something else in your life other than your stupid murals. Is that why you're fooling around with that guy?"

"Oh my god, will you stop that? I'm not fooling around with him."

"Yeah, right. The way you've been acting, and . . . those jeans you were wearing . . ."

"Those jeans mean nothing."

"You tell Dad the truth, or I will," I threaten.

She drops her cigarette into a coffee cup. It sizzles in the pooled dregs.

Her phone buzzes. She doesn't answer—doesn't even look at it.

"Is that him? Is that Mike?"

She closes her eyes.

"Go ahead. . . . Answer it. I don't care. I don't care anymore what you do." I run upstairs, take a quick shower—douse my hair with her expensive olive oil—line my eyes with dark, heavy makeup, slip on a maxi dress, jean jacket, and cowboy boots, and grab a suitcase from my closet. *I'll move in with Chris. That's what I'll do. I can't stay here any longer, with her lying to me, to Dad. . . . I can't.*

My phone rings. It's Chris:

Me: I was just thinking about you . . .
Chris: *Bea.*

Me: I can hardly hear you. You okay?
Chris: No. I'm hurt. I got jumped.
Me: What? Oh my god! Where are you?
Chris: St. Joe's. Emergency. Please. Come.

1 day
4 hours
40 minutes

I rush into St. Joseph's emergency room and am instantly hit with the thick air of pain, worry, and sadness. A family huddles in the corner, crying deep, gut-level sobs. An old lady, who doesn't smell exactly fresh, is sprawled on two plastic chairs, sleeping, snoring away, plastic bags packed with stuff tightly clutched in her hands. A man in a hospital gown is yelling at the receptionist, "I've been waiting for three hours!"

I approach a nurse . . . or doctor. I have no idea who this woman is, but she acts important—wears a white coat and carries a clipboard.

"I'm looking for a patient. Chris Mayes."

"Uh-huh." She walks fast across the speckled tile floor of the hallway.

I follow. "He's been beat up. I don't know where he is."

"Bea?" I hear a weak voice coming from down the hall, ten feet ahead.

Chris sits upright on a gurney in the hallway, his bare legs dangling. Half of his head is patched with blood-stained gauze. The other side of his blond hair is tinted red.

I rush to him. Hug him. "Chris."

"Ouch." He winces.

I pull back. "What happened? Who did this to you?"

"I'm okay, Bea. It looks worse than it is. Just a couple cuts they had to stitch up—thankfully, it was the short side, 'cause they had to buzz it."

"But there's so much blood."

"They said the head bleeds a lot, I guess. And I'm waiting for them to X-ray my ribs."

The blood, the smell . . . makes me want to throw up.

The disgust must register on my face because Chris says, "I'm sorry I called you."

"No. No. Don't be sorry. I'm here for you. What can I do? You need something?"

"A ride home? They've given me some stuff. I don't think I should drive."

"Oh, yeah, sure, of course. But what about your parents?"

"Thank god I'm eighteen. They didn't have to call them. No way will they understand. I'll tell them I fell off the uneven bars, trying out for gymnastics, or something."

"Yeah. Right. That'll fly. . . . You fell into shards of glass."

"Bea. Stop. Please, don't make jokes."

"What about Ian?"

"We broke up."

190

"What? Oh, no . . ."

"Yeah, I think that hurts more than my wounds. He needs space, he said."

"Oh, Chris." I gingerly hug him. "Who beat you up? Tell me."

He covers his face with his hand. "It all happened so fast. I messed up. I should have listened to you. I shouldn't have said anything . . . but I had to. He was in the library, holding court, bragging about his stupid SAT score."

"No, Chris, don't tell me . . . Zac . . ."

"I was so upset with the Ian thing. I wasn't thinking straight."

"What did you say?"

"I didn't say I knew. I whispered something stupid like, 'Why don't we ask Billy what he thinks about your score?'"

My stomach drops. "Oh, no . . . why did I tell you? I never should've."

"It happened really fast. All I remember is that I was in the school parking lot, unlocking my car, and then something crashed over my head. I think it was a glass bottle, and I guess I went down when he kicked me. I remember crawling into the driver's seat, and I somehow got my ass here."

"Mayes. Chris Mayes?" A guy in a blue uniform calls out.

"Here." Chris raises his hand like it's roll call at school.

The orderly walks over. "We'll be taking you up to radiation for an X-ray soon. Lie back," he orders.

Chris does, holding onto my hand as if we're in one of those sappy movies—like he's going into some major surgery and was given crappy odds. He's rolled ten feet into a sterile room, with three curtained-off cubicles. An old man moans through the thin curtain; he's mumbling something about Jell-O.

A girl—I think I recognize her from rehab last summer, but hope not, because she's totally high out of her mind, laughing and dancing with her curtain as if it's a ball gown, exposing her butt cheeks, chewing a wad of tobacco, and spitting onto the floor. "Isn't this friggin' amazing? It's like, oh my god, I love the music."

There's no music playing.

We reach Chris's designated corner. I sit on a folding chair, try to make myself comfortable—impossible, to say the least.

Chris's bottom lip quivers. Tears drip down his cheeks. I lean over and wipe them with a tissue.

"I loved Ian."

I squeeze his hand. "I know you did, but he's not good enough for you. You're going to meet a ton of hotties at school and you won't want to be attached to a high schooler . . . it'll be open season for you."

He forces the corners of his mouth to curl. "You're probably right . . . as always."

"But, that ass, Zac. . . . I feel like killing him, or hiring someone to beat the crap out of him." A fabulous fantasy flashes through my mind for a second: Reyna and Roxanne rabidly chewing, gnawing on his bloody carcass.

"Leave it alone, Bea. Like you told me to. He's a monster. I don't want you to get hurt, too."

No way am I going to leave it alone; no way.

The old man suddenly yells, "And whip cream on top, the fresh kind. None of that Cool Whip stuff."

A girl who looks younger than me parts the curtain. "Hi. I'm Dr. Mendez." She introduces herself. "And you are?"

I stand, towering over her, and I'm only five foot five. "I'm Beatrice Washington. And this is my best friend Chris Mayes."

"Very nice to meet you both."

"Is he okay?" I barrel past the how-do-you-do's.

She leafs through what I assume is his chart—a clipboard filled with three inches of paper.

"Hasn't he only been here a couple hours? I mean, what are you doing? Don't look at those papers . . . look at him."

"Bea, stop," Chris pleads. "Let the doctor do her job."

Dr. Mendez ignores me. "Mr. Mayes, I'm going to ask you to roll over to your left side. From what this paperwork says"—she throws that in my face at a speed of ninety miles per hour—"it seems one of your ribs may be bruised—hopefully not fractured."

Chris complies, winces.

"Please, Bea," he whispers. "Don't tell anyone he did this. Please, let it go."

I lean into my friend and hold his hand, kiss his tears.

The doc finishes her exam. "The orderly will bring you up

to radiology. It'll take about an hour," she says in a brusque tone, and disappears through the curtain.

"You'll wait here, right, Bea? You'll stay?"

"Of course. I'm not going anywhere." The orderly whips open the curtain, raises the railing on Chris's bed, and starts rolling him out of the room.

I peek in on the old man. "I'll check on the Jell-O."

"Whip cream," he yells as I leave the room, "the real stuff!"

"Annie?" I part the curtain. She's sleeping. I read her clipboard hung on the base of her bed. *Damn*. It is her. The Annie from rehab. Her drug of choice was heroin, smack. She's one of the nice ones, incredibly sweet when she was sober. And smart—damn, she was one of the most well-read teens I've ever met. She loves poetry and quoted Emily Dickinson all the time. Not in a snobbish way—she just got it, life, deeper than anybody else.

It's that depth, the ability to touch stuff that most don't see, don't even know is there. . . . It's scary, lonely, and can take you down into the hole.

I've never met a stupid addict.

• • •

I have an hour and really want to see Junior since I'm already here, so I hustle to the intensive care unit. It's shaped like a horseshoe. Pods jut out—the rooms of the most critically ill.

The sound of machines beeping; low, concerned voices; soft weeping. The smell in the air is thick with the sweet stench of rubbing alcohol, spilled guts, worry, and grief.

A man in blue scrubs approaches—he could be a doctor, a surgeon, or he could be in housekeeping. I'm sure it matters to him, but it doesn't to me.

"Hello. I'm here to see Junior," I say, realizing for the first time that I don't know his last name, or even if his real name is Junior.

He points to the third door on the left. "Are you family?"

I nod, kind of in a circle. Could be interpreted both ways. "How is he?"

"He's been in and out of consciousness since surgery. We're waiting for the swelling to go down, and won't know what we're looking at for a couple days."

He's a doctor, I gather, or a very well-informed janitor.

"But he already has visitors. You'll have to wait," he adds.

"Oh, okay. That's fine."

He gestures toward a line of stacked chairs against a wall. I thank him and take a seat across from Junior's pod.

His curtain is closed shut across the glass. The nurse sits on a stool, taking notes. I'm sure he's interpreting the flashing numbers, the graph-lined screen in front of him.

The beeping of one of the machines suddenly picks up, and the nurse enters Junior's room, swings back the curtain, and I see him, lying in the bed. His head bandaged, wrapped; his body motionless. Reyna, Archie, Johnny, Roxanne, and a couple kids from the team I haven't met yet, along with Coach, the gold chains on his wrist glistening, surround him.

The nurse speaks with the coach. He listens with a concerned face. Then he nods, and the group rises. Reyna kisses Junior on the cheek. They're silent, heads lowered. Roxanne wipes tears away as they walk toward the exit, toward me.

Damn . . . they're going to see me. I slump, covering my face with my hand, and then realize that I don't have to. *I'm dressed like a girl—Bea, not Boy.* I relax, nod as they pass, and then oh my friggin' god, I sneeze.

The coach stops for a beat, looks at me. "Bless you."

Fuck! I mumble back a thank-you and wait patiently on the hard-backed chair until the nurse settles back on the stool. "Is it okay if I go in now?"

"Only for a couple minutes—that's it," he says to me. "Please keep him calm. We don't want to upset him."

"Of course. But will he be able to hear me?"

"We think so. He's not able to speak yet, but he's been responding to basic commands."

"That's good, right?"

"It's a good sign, yes."

"So he'll be okay?"

"The swelling's gone down, but it's still too soon to tell."

I head into the room. "Hi, Junior." I sit on a chair next to his bed. A lightweight tube that splits into two prongs hangs from his nostrils; lines reach from his arms to bloated baggies with fluid that hang on a T-shaped roller; patches on his chest are connected to a machine with colorful squiggly lines. The beeping of the machines is steady, slow, strong.

He looks peaceful, his handsome face relaxed. "Junior, I don't know if you can hear me or if you even remember me, but I'm the girl who was pretending to be a boy, the one in the holding cell with you that day. My name is Bea. Beatrice Washington. I wanted to tell you that I'm sorry." My voice trips with sudden emotion. "I didn't know what the tennis balls meant. I'm so sorry I ratted on you. I really didn't know."

Junior's swollen, heavy lids struggle to open.

"You can hear me!" I sit straighter, take his hand in mine.

He makes a grunting noise, and taps my hand with his finger.

"What, what is it?"

The beeping picks up on the monitor.

"I was told not to get you upset. I should go."

I start to stand, and he reaches out, brushes my hand. I sit back down and he lifts his finger again. But this time he moves it around in the air, like it's a pencil, like he's . . .

"Drawing? You want me to draw something? Okay." I pull my sketchbook and a pen out of my bag.

Junior's eyes open a bit wider, and I peer into the wet darkness of his eyes, and instantly letters come marching in, rolling like a combination on a lock: I-S-P-Y. I look down at what I wrote. "ISPY? What does this mean, Junior? What are you trying to tell me?"

His heart rate, the beeps, suddenly pick up speed—race. The lines on the machine fluctuate in waves—high and low. The nurse runs in the room, swiftly ushers me out, and closes the curtain.

1 day
1 hour
12 minutes

A rm in arm, we shuffle in the rain through the heavily-lit hospital parking lot. I hold my jean jacket over Chris's head (I forgot an umbrella and make a mental note to add one to the collection in my backseat), so as not to get his bandage wet.

"Hey, instead of driving me home, do you think I could stay with you for a while, at your house? Please?" Chris asks, his voice muffled under the jacket.

"Of course." I help him sit in the car, wrap the safety belt around his sore ribs, and buckle him up, and then run around to the other side of the car and jump in. "Whew." I wipe my face with my hands, fluff my hands through my hair. "You should probably let your parents know where you are."

"Yeah, I know. I'll tell them I'm with you, studying or something, but nothing else. Believe me, they don't want to know. They never want to know the truth about me. It'll be

199

easier for them, for me, if I hide out for a while. I'll sleep on the floor. I won't be a problem, I promise."

I pull out onto the street, my windshield wipers working hard. "You're not going to sleep on the floor. You know I have a queen bed."

"Perfect." He laughs. Stops, holds his side in pain. "Oh, shit, but Zac . . . he's your neighbor. What if he sees me?"

"He's not going to see you; don't worry. I don't think he's ever stepped foot in my yard." *And he better not.* "But you need to know, it's pretty tense at my house. My mom and I aren't talking. I was actually about to go to your house, before you called from the hospital."

"Yeah, right. The two of you don't know how *not* to talk."

"It's a rule I just made up. I don't want to talk to her again for the rest of my life."

"I'll believe it when I see it. What are you going to say, or not say, about bringing home a pulverized pal?" he asks.

"The truth. That a douche bag phony asshole jerk beat you up."

"Well, that's one way of putting it."

• • •

"Are you sure you don't need a heating pad for your ribs?" my mom asks, propping Chris up with a third pillow, covering him with yet another blanket.

I stand at my bathroom sink, brushing my teeth. "He's

going to die of heatstroke, Mom. Stop covering him! They said ice. Where's Dad by the way?"

"Working late again. How about I make us some hot tea." She tucks in the side of the quilt.

I spit in the sink. "For chrissakes, leave him alone. He's fine."

Chris, looking stiff and uncomfortable, sits straight up at a ninety-degree angle in my bed, listening to the two of us bicker. "I'm really okay, thank you. And thanks for letting me stay here."

"You're always welcome. You know that. And hopefully under better circumstances next time." She stands at the door of my room, like she's waiting for an invitation to jump on the bed.

"It's late, Mom. I think Chris should get some sleep." I gently pull one of the pillows out from behind him and untuck the quilt.

"Well, he's not going to school in the morning, that's for sure. He'll stay here; I'll take care of him. I'm free, don't have anything planned." She darts her eyes at me.

"But *I* have to get up for school, so would you mind leaving, please?"

"Okay. Good night." She starts to close the door, then pokes her head back in. "I'm down the hall if you need anything."

"Mom."

Door closed. I switch off the light. The almost full moon shines through the thick clouds, casting a filtered, hazy, almost spooky glow through the window and into my room—perfect for a scary-story sleepover. But the scary story tonight happens to be real.

"I think you made her day, getting beat up. I guess it's good to bring in a busted-up buddy now and then to ease the tension in a dysfunctional family."

"Tell me about dysfunctional families . . . mine can trump yours any day."

I plop down on the bed with him.

"Easy, Bea." He winces.

"Oh, sorry." I slowly sit up, lean against the headboard. "It'll get better, your family, when you get out of the house, go to school. You'll see."

"Yeah, I guess. I'd hate to have to lie to my parents the rest of my life." He gingerly rolls to his side, faces me. "By the way, I told ya so."

"Told me what?"

"There's no silent treatment going on between you two."

I fold my arms. "Well, there should be."

"Why, what happened, anyway?"

"She's fooling around on my dad, Chris. There's another guy. A stupid-looking dude with a moustache."

"No. No way."

"Yes way. It pisses me off, and I feel so bad for my dad. I don't think he has any idea."

"Well, that sucks."

I scooch down under the covers, cuddle up next to him. Our faces are inches apart.

"This is kind of fun," he says.

"Fun? You've been beaten to a pulp, my mom is having an affair, and you find this fun?"

"Having a sleepover with you."

"Yeah, okay, that part is fun. But we should try it again, without the drama next time—I'd prefer ghost stories and s'mores."

"You know, Bea. We *could* get an apartment, live together, after my freshman year."

I sigh. "We could, and I'd be up for that. But Chris, you're going to meet new people—your whole life will probably change. And that's fine. It is. We'll always be close—forever, I know it. Don't worry about me, okay?"

"Okay, but I do." His smile fades. "My pain pills are in my jeans pocket, you know."

I lift my head, look across the room at his pants draped over the back of a chair. "I know. I saw them."

"You're cool with it?"

I gently entwine my fingers around his hand. "Life is weird."

"How so?"

"Even when things get scary messy—you getting beat up by that jerk . . ." *And everything that's happened with Junior.* "You're handed a moment like this. Just the two of us, in this room. The moon shining in. It's so peaceful."

"That sounds rather sappy. So un-Bea-like."

"Shut up. I'm just grateful that I'm here to help you, and that you asked me to. It wouldn't have happened if I were messed up—we wouldn't have this moment. So, yeah, Chris, that's a long way of saying I'm cool with the pills in your pocket. Good night." I kiss him on the cheek, roll over, lace up the imaginary boxing gloves, and say a prayer for Annie.

But I don't sleep. I hear the minutes ticking by, Chris's light snores. I'm afraid to move, disturb him, and my mind keeps switching on and off, flashing between the image of Junior, lying in that hospital bed, and then to that asshole Zac, and what he did to Chris.

And the letters I-S-P-Y . . . What was Junior trying to tell me? ISPY, I SPY, I spy . . . Oh my god . . . *The tattoo on the coach's Adam's apple—an eye spying . . . of course. Junior wanted me to know, confirmed my hunch—it's Coach Credos—no doubt about it.*

I slowly, silently slip out from under the covers, tiptoe to my closet, close the door. It's only eleven thirty; he should be up. I dial his number. But I get Sergeant Daniels's message instead and whisper into the phone:

Me: It's the coach, Dan, I'm positive. I saw Junior at
    the hospital and drew the truth out of him . . . the
    coach's eye tattoo—it's what he was thinking about—
    what he wanted me to know.

"**M**r. Pogen? You need help passing out the graded tests?"

"Sure, Beatrice, that would be nice." He hands me the stack.

I shuffle through the pile, pull out Zac's and Chris's, and stuff them in my purse. "Um, I'll take Chris's home to him. He's not feeling well today." I shoot a deadly glance toward the asshole.

"That'd be nice, thank you. Now remember, class, don't forget to bring this when we take the final. Use it—it's all there—everything you need to know. And those of you who didn't do so well, please redo the work at home. If you need help, come see me. I want you all to be prepared."

"Uh, I didn't get mine back," Zac utters, his big, lunky body squeezed into a desk. Sometimes I wish he'd get stuck in one and have to walk around the school wearing it like a wooden tutu.

"Oh, that's odd. Beatrice? Was it in the stack?"

"Nope, didn't see it," I lie.

"Well, meet me after class, Zac. I'll have a look around. By the way, you didn't do too well. We'll have to make sure you're up to speed for the final."

The class snickers. Zac's face morphs into the swollen red hive-y thing again—he's *so* not fooling anyone.

And he won't ever again.

It came to me the moment I woke in the morning and looked at Chris's innocent face—his bandaged head. How to take Zac down . . .

I had to let go of the Reyna/Roxanne she-wolf evisceration. It was a juicy fantasy that I wallowed around in for a while. I also considered calling Johnny and Archie, asking them to meet up with him in a dark alley somewhere as mean thugs, and scare the crap out of him—not hurt him, but tap into their gangsta mojo. They would love to do that, I'm sure, and Zac would've probably pooped his pants on the spot. But I can't risk getting them in trouble with the coach, and there's no way I'd stoop to his level, using violence as an answer.

And then it came to me: Jeremy, his little brother. He's the one who should, who has to, who *will* . . . take his big brother down.

"Jeremy." I run to his locker. He stands slumped, defeated as always, pulling out books.

"What do you want?"

I hand him a stamped envelope addressed: The College Board, Office of Testing Integrity.

He studies it, front and back. "What's this?"

"Look inside." He pulls out the failed astronomy test.

"That's your brother's signature." I point at the top of the page.

"Okay . . . what am I supposed to do with it?"

"Anything you want."

"Huh?"

I lean in, whisper, "There's some suspicion, rumors floating around, that maybe, perhaps, your big brother had someone else take the SAT for him."

Oh man, I wish I had Chris's camera—the expression on Jeremy's face . . . priceless. His dull gray eyes widened, his slack, beardless jaw clenched, his shoulders pulled back, and I watched him suddenly grow two inches taller. "You're shitting me."

"I'm not. One look at his academic record, the differences with the signatures, no way they'll ignore it—they'll at least investigate."

He leans his head against the top shelf of his locker and deflates a little. "But I couldn't do that . . . no way, I couldn't. I can't blow his dream . . . I'm not like him."

"But you don't have to, you see? All he needs to know is that you possess the power, right there in your hands, to put him in his place." I repeat this part slowly. "You'd have the power, Jeremy."

He slowly turns his head and smiles at me, and it occurs to me that I've never seen his smile before. "I would, wouldn't I?"

"You would. And, anyway, he's not going to be able to fool Cornell University. No way will he get through a quarter, let alone a semester."

Zac comes stalking toward us. "What you doin' talking to her?" he asks, and then shoves the locker door hard into Jeremy's back. He continues marching down the hall, yuk-yukking like a fool.

Jeremy's nostrils flare, and it seems as if he taps into *his* superpower as he fills up his skinny body with air and shouts out, "Hey, Zachary!"

His brother whirls around, storms over. "I told you, never to talk to me here, you got that?"

"No, I got this." He holds up the envelope. Zac snatches it from his hand, pulls out the folded test.

"So?" He shifts his weight in his size twenty sneakers.

"So, look at the address."

He does, followed by the neck spasm thing.

"That's your signature, right, on the test? The same signature you wrote when you signed in for the SAT?"

Zac snarls, rips the envelope, the test in half, in quarters, shoves the pieces in his pocket.

Jeremy blinks at me, like, *Now what?*

I pull out another stamped, addressed envelope from within the pages of my sketchbook. "I figured you'd do that. Unless you weren't worried about Jeremy sending in your signature.

But just in case, I happened to have made a copy of the test." I hand it to Jeremy. "Oh, yeah. . . . I made a few copies, actually."

Zac tries to snatch it again, but Jeremy, faster this time, tosses it in his locker, slams the door closed, and spins the lock.

Zac makes a guttural noise and raises a clenched fist above his brother's head.

I step in, ready to take the blow, grab the collar of his shirt, and growl back, "You touch him or Chris, talk shit to Billy, to anyone, ever again, and I'll take you down, you little lying prick—and you know I will."

His fist lowers.

"Believe me, I'll be watching you."

8 hours
15 minutes

knock on his office door.

"Bea. What are you doing here? I mean, not that I'm not glad to see you."

I sit on an upholstered wingback chair across from the polished, dark wood desk. "I have to tell you something, Dad. I've debated, thought it over and over, but I do. I have to tell you the truth."

He sits, his hands clasped atop his desk. "This sounds very important."

"It is. And it's about Mom." Big breath. "She's seeing someone else, Dad. She's cheating on you."

He cups the back of his neck, drops his head.

"I'm sorry. So sorry. But I thought you'd want to know."

"Bea . . ."

A light knock on the door. A young woman with a brown, messy ponytail, wearing black, thick-framed glasses that teeter on the tip of her cute-as-a-button nose, comes rushing in—then stops short when she sees me. "Oh . . ."

My dad jumps up, briskly crosses over to her. "I don't think this is a good time . . ."

"Hi." I wave.

"Bea, this is Professor Williams. She's a painting teacher here at the university. And Marcy, um, Professor Williams, this is my daughter, Beatrice." He unbuttons the top button on his shirt, loosens his tie.

"Nice to meet you, Beatrice. I've heard a lot about you." Her high cheekbones flush as she quickly places a folder on Dad's desk. "I need to get your approval with these order forms . . . when you have time. Okay, bye. Nice meeting you." She waves and scoots out of the room.

Dad wipes his sweaty forehead, faces me, and it looks as if he's wearing a mask. A mask I've never seen before on his face. I've seen it on my mom's, plenty of times—the mask of guilt. The sallow, blood-draining, empty-eyed look of guilt.

It explodes, bursts like a popped balloon, a rubber band *snap*. And I'm not drawing—no pen, no paper in hand. *No, no, no. This can't be true.*

He kneels at my chair as if he's in a confessional. Puts his hands on my lap. "Your mother isn't having an affair, Beatrice."

I shove his hands off me, then jump up. "Oh my god . . . it's you, you're the one?"

"Bea." He stays in a kneeling position . . . as he should.

"All this time, I thought it was Mom who was the fraud,

the phony. But I was wrong. It was you." I have the urge to push his stupid-ass desk over as I rush past him to the door. "I've got to get out of here. I've got to get to Mom."

"Bea. Please, come back. I can explain. . . ."

"Don't bother," I call back.

• • •

I find Chris and my mom in her bed, watching TV. They're both still in pj's and are laughing their asses off at an animal-prank show, munching on a big bowl of popcorn.

"That pug. Did you see that, what he did with that turtle? Ow, my ribs. Stop it. Turn it off. . . . It hurts too much to laugh." Chris rolls to his side, hysterical.

"Oh, honey, be careful," Mom says, and adjusts the ice pack underneath him. She glances up at me in the doorway. "Oh, hi, Bea." It's as unwelcoming a greeting as an unpopped kernel at the bottom of the bowl—the thing you spit out and discard. And I don't blame her, with what I've said, the way I've acted.

I sit on Chris's side of the bed. "How you feeling, buddy?"

"Oh, man, Bea, wow . . . I finally get it."

"What?"

"What you saw in all the drugs you took. . . . Hell, I'm in no pain. No pain at all," he slurs. "And your mom, she's like a goddess, she made me an omelet this morning that, no way—never have I ever tasted anything so delish."

Enjoying my mom's food? He's so high.

"Hey, Mom, can we talk?"

She stands, wraps her robe tightly around her body, I'm sure bracing for another onslaught. "Go ahead."

"I mean alone."

"Oh, girl talk, fine, I know when I'm not wanted." Chris scrambles off the bed. "I have to take a shower, anyway, wash my lovely half head of hair."

"Be careful of the bandages," Mom warns.

"I will . . . oh, and Bea, would you mind driving me home in a little bit? I'll get my car another day, when I'm not feeling . . . whoozy." He wobbles.

"Good idea, Chris." I hold on to his arm and walk him to the door.

When he leaves, I close the door and rush to my mom and hug her tightly, so tightly—she stumbles backward.

"Whoa. What's that for?"

I start bawling. "I'm sorry. I thought it was you, not Dad."

"What are you talking about?"

"I went to his office, and that woman, the Marcy woman, came in . . ."

"Ahhh . . ." She pulls me into her even tighter, rocks me back and forth. "You found out." I nod in her bosom. She steps back, pets my hair, takes my face in her hands. "You okay?"

"How could he?"

"Bea, he's not a bad person."

"How can you say that? How long has this been going on? How long have you known?"

She shrugs. "I think this Professor Williams thing has been going on for a while. . . . It may be getting pretty serious. Your dad's been coming home later and later—sometimes he doesn't even bother."

I sink onto the bed. "Why didn't you tell me?"

"I didn't want to hurt you." She hands me a box of Kleenex.

"How can you live in this house with him?" I ask, wiping my face.

"Because you're here." She sits on the bed with me. "I loved your father, Bea, I did, you have to know that. And I know I'm not easy to live with."

"But, that's no excuse . . . what he's doing."

"I know, but we met very young; he was lost, I was lost, and both of us were passionate and stubborn—we had no idea what we were doing in life. And we fell deeply in love. I don't regret any of it, because we had you." She kisses my forehead. "And all was good, for a long while. You remember that, right? Good times?"

I nod. "But that Mr. Connelly . . ."

"Michael? He's a client—that's it. Yeah, we flirted. . . . It felt kind of good to be appreciated."

I blow my nose. "Was he here with you? Last week? The morning I came home?"

"What? Of course not."

"But I saw his truck . . ."

"Bea, he wasn't here, believe me. Do you know how many white SUVs are out there?"

214

SNITCH

"And you were acting so guilty, like I caught you doing something."

She stands, crosses over to her vanity. "The truth? I was." She pulls open the top drawer, fingers a few cigarettes. "I was having a smoke up here. I told you I've been lifting them off you. I didn't want you to know . . . that is, until you got me fired."

"That's it? That's all you were doing?"

"I know, pretty lame, right?" She sits.

"Oh my god . . . I'm sorry, Mom. I'm so sorry I lost you your job."

"It's okay. I never would've made Alanna happy."

I slap the bed. "You can't live this way, Mom. You're beautiful, smart, and you look fabulous in those jeans, by the way."

She smiles. "Thank you."

"You deserve more."

She peers at me through the mirror. "You know, when I went to see my parents, your grandparents, on Sunday, it felt good to be . . ." She sighs. "Home. They're willing to forgive and forget—everything, all the drama, the fights, the silence between us. And I am, too." She pauses. "They want me to move back."

"What?" I hold a pillow close to my chest. "To Chicago? With them?"

"After you graduate, of course, if that's what you want, or . . . we could go now."

"Now? As in *now*?"

215

She swings around. "I told them all about you. How talented, smart, and beautiful you are. Oh, Bea . . . they would love to get to know you. You could even finish the school year there if you wanted. I know you never liked Packard High. We could start . . . fresh. Just the two of us."

I'm silent.

"Or not. It's up to you." She begins writing in a card.

"What are you doing?"

"I'm finishing up a thank-you note." She laughs. "They don't understand e-mail . . . one of the first things I'll help them with when I move."

When. She said *when.* I look at her in the mirror—happily mouthing the words as she writes, and I think, *Why shouldn't we pack up and leave? Why not? What do I have here? I don't want to ever see my dad again, Chris will be moving on, but Dan . . . Sergeant Daniels. God. I can't imagine never seeing those green eyes again.*

"You really care about him, don't you?" She's eyeing me through the mirror.

"What, who?"

She swivels in her chair, faces me. "Whoever belongs to these eyes—they don't really look like Wendell's." She hands me the note card. A pair of eyes—the shape, the intensity of Sergeant Daniels's eyes perfectly drawn at the top. "Who is he? Are you in love with him?"

I stand. "Mom . . . how did you . . ."

"I'm your mom, I know things, I see things."

"No. No. That isn't it. You . . . drew what I was thinking."

"You mean the truth?" She hands me the pen, the note card. "Now it's your turn."

"What?"

"It's okay, Bea. Don't be scared." Her dark eyes take hold of mine, lassoing them, pulling them into hers. A memory surfaces, circles around, somersaults back to when I was a little girl in braids, in the Chicago loft . . .

We were sitting at the kitchen table. It was summertime and hot. A ceiling fan twirled above, blowing her long, wavy hair into her face as she painted a portrait of me for my dad's birthday. "Shhhh . . . we're going to keep it a secret, okay, Bea?"

I sat across from her, my little legs stuck with sweat on the plastic chair. I was having a hard time keeping still, and squirmed a lot.

"Baby, come on. Try and stay put. Daddy's going to be home soon."

But I was hot and sad; all I wanted to do was cry. I kept thinking about swimming camp earlier that day at the local Y. Cindy Pritchett passed out invitations to her birthday party during break time. All the girls were giggling, waiting, dripping, wrapped in long towels. I never got one. She passed right by me.

"You know, I never did like that Cindy girl," Mom said out of the blue. "I don't even know if I'd *want* to go to a party of hers. She's so snotty."

"But Mommy, I didn't tell you about Cindy's party. How did you know I wasn't invited?"

She rubbed her forehead, smeared a splotch of yellow paint between her brows. "You didn't?"

Dad burst into the apartment. "I got it, Bella. I got it, Beatrice." He swooped me up into his arms. "You're looking at the next Chair of the Art Department at the University of Michigan." Mom joined the hug.

We started packing right then and there. The birthday portrait forgotten; Cindy Pritchett's party forgotten . . . until now.

"Mom."

"What am I thinking? Draw it on that paper. Draw the truth out of me. Go ahead."

And it tumbles in like marbles . . . steely metal balls, touching, clicking—an unstrung abacus, balls hitting one another—the numbers rolling like dice on a crap table. The number three pops in my head. My hand trembles as I scratch it out. The number six, and then the number eight. I look down at the card, puzzled.

She lifts my chin, meets my eyes with hers, and I've never seen her face like this—so relaxed. No sign of the worry vein splitting it in two. "It's the combination on the lock above the fridge."

I speak without breathing. "You, too?"

She sits, almost collapsing back down on her vanity chair. "I can't hide anymore, Bea. I'm almost forty. I'm tired of running away from it all."

"But . . . you knew about me, *it*, when?"

"When you left your astronomy book out on the kitchen counter. There was a very good rendering of Michael's moustache. You knew I was thinking of him, texting him. I almost said something to you that night . . . but I wasn't sure. And I was afraid."

"Afraid of what?"

"That it was true."

I sink down on the bed. "But . . . Dad, I thought all this time, because he stopped drawing . . ."

"He stopped for exactly the reason he said. He had to concentrate on making a living for us. And he wasn't a very good artist, by the way—but don't tell him I said that." A little laugh. "Not that he would care what I think."

"Does he know, about you—what you can do?"

"No. He'd probably think I was drinking again."

"So when did it happen for you, Mom?"

"When I got sober—is that when . . ."

She doesn't have to complete the question. "Yes, yes, I thought I was crazy. Thought I was going mad." I cover my face with her pillow. *My mom? She has this power, too? She's the one? Why didn't she tell me, warn me? Like, oh, by the way, you may be an addict, and may have a freaky paranormal ability. Just wanted you to know, in case it happens to you, too, when you grow up.* I slap the pillow on my lap. "I don't understand. Why didn't you say anything? I thought I was nuts. Don't you think you should have said something to me?"

She stands. "I've tried not to think about it. I shut it down awhile ago."

"And me with it."

"I'm sorry. I know what a burden it is. I'm sorry you take after me. If I would have known, I . . ."

"What? You wouldn't have had me?"

"Oh my god, no. You're the best thing that ever happened to me—the most honest part of my life." She pulls me into her, hugs me, almost breaking *my* ribs. "You're stronger than me, Bea, and have found good in all the bad that's been handed to you. I've hid from it. It's why I've faced the wall all these years when I paint, but you, you've faced it straight on. You've given me the courage, the reason to stay sober all these years."

I pull away. "But that wasn't supposed to be my job, Mom. That was yours. I'm the kid; you're the adult."

"Fair enough." She stands straight. "And it's time I grew up, and about time I let you, too. So that apartment? Whatever you decide to do—live with me, near me, wherever . . . I will support you in your decision. I believe in you, Bea. I trust you."

"You do?"

"I do. Aren't you going to see what's in the cabinet?"

"What? What are you talking about?"

"Your birthday present. You have the code."

I bolt down the stairs, pull a chair over, dial in the numbers, and see that the scotch, the medications, the vanilla extract are gone, and instead it's filled with journals. A half dozen leather-backed, worn journals stacked neatly in a pile. I grab one, leaf through. They are filled with sketches, amazing renderings of people, things, half-drawn objects—and Mom's maiden name scrawled at the top of each one . . . *Annabelle Francesca Scavo.*

"It's time I meet up with that young woman again." Her voice cracks.

Chris walks in, wearing my baby-blue terry robe and matching slippers (last year's birthday gift). The long side of his hair is slicked down like a wet seal, and he's holding the spritz bottle of olive oil. "What the hell, Bea. . . . I thought this was product." The room reeks of extra virgin olive oil.

Mom's eyes narrow at me. "Is that where it went?"

I shrug, step off the stool. "You could've always drawn it out of me."

6 hours
25 minutes

drive home from Chris's and see him, Sergeant Dan Daniels, following me in my rearview mirror, and laugh. Thank goodness he's not flashing his lights. I slowly pull over to the side of the road.

Instead of license and registration, he says, "Can I buy you a pop?"

We sit in a booth at a diner—same booth we sat in over six months ago, the first time I knew I was tumbling headfirst into the *shouldn't* storm—into his Caribbean Sea green eyes.

"So, what happened with Coach Credos? Did you check out the ceiling tiles?"

"Yes, we did. We found the booze—that's it. He nips at the bottle, but there was nothing illegal, absolutely nothing."

I stir my Coke with the straw, fast, creating a whirlpool in the tall glass. "But it all adds up, the eye tattoo on his neck. When I saw Junior in the hospital . . . that's what he was thinking about—an eye, spying. It's what I drew." I pull out my Moleskine and show him the letters. "Junior was trying to tell me that it was Credos."

"I'm sorry, but . . ."

"I know he's guilty; I know it." I slam my hand on the table.

"Bea . . ." He puts his hand on top of mine. "There's something else."

"Why do I think I'm not going to like this?"

"I wanted to tell you in person that I'm looking into moving to Chicago to be closer to Max. I'm hoping to get a position at a precinct—maybe a lateral transfer."

Oh my god, this would be so perfect . . . I could move with my mom, and everything would be okay—we'd be together. This is so friggin' awesome!

"And"—he removes his hand from mine and rearranges the utensils, straightens the napkins on the table—"I've been thinking long and hard about you and me." He leans in. "I shouldn't be using you the way I do, your *drawing* thing. It isn't right. I don't think we should, um, see each other anymore."

"What?" I push into the quilted back of the booth. "No, no!" I shake my head. "It's okay; I don't mind you using me. I didn't mean what I said before—at the courthouse."

"Bea, it's too risky, and Detective Cole . . . he's been asking a lot of questions."

"Who cares about him? And if we move to Chicago, it won't matter."

"What? What do you mean *we*?"

"Is it because I haven't cracked the case? Is that why?" I hold back tears.

"Bea, no . . ."

I stand. "You know, I really have to go. I have something to do. . . . Let's talk about this later, okay?"

I run out to my car. My eyes sting, my ears are ringing, my throat feels raw. *I can't lose him; I can't. I have to prove to him that he needs me.*

I text Archie:

ME: down with the tridge. what time are u and johnny meeting?

5 hours
45 minutes

pull on the baggy jeans, and don't bother flattening my chest because I'm planning to keep the hoodie on. It's a chilly fifty-something and going to get cooler as the night goes on. And to make the prep even easier? I don't have to twist or gel my hair because Johnny suggested I bring a ski mask if I had one, saying it's good to keep our faces covered because we'll be upside down, spraying. *Upside down?*

I found one in the front closet in a bag filled with mothballs, labeled ski stuff. The memory cracked me up and punched me in the gut at the same time. We went skiing, as a family . . . once . . . at Boyne Highlands resort up north. This was before my druggie days, so I had no excuse, other than being a klutz, for having to be tobogganed by the paramedics down one of the slopes after getting my skis tangled coming off the ski lift. They dug into the snow, and I fell over sideways. The next group slid right over me, and the next, and the next, until my mom's screaming convinced the lift operator to finally shut it down. My dad helped me to a vertical position as everyone dangled above, swaying back and forth, watching the girl dressed like the Michelin man scramble to her feet, only to fall again and slide directly into a tree.

I spent the whole day at the local urgent care, waiting for my ankle to be X-rayed, sitting, sweating in a wet woolen sweater that itched like crazy, listening to my parents bicker about who was responsible for letting me fall. It ended up only being a sprained ankle, but my ego was bruised enough to prevent me from ever hitting the slopes again.

Yeah, those were the good old days.

The face mask stinks, but I pull it on, bunch the face part up on my forehead, and I'm good to go.

We meet at Depot Town in Ypsilanti: a restored historic railroad station a couple blocks from the courthouse—the *usual place* with Daniels.

We sit, waiting for Johnny, at the side of the Amtrak train tracks running southeast toward Jackson. Spiky dandelions and splotches of grass struggle to bloom between the railroad ties. *Ballsy of them*, I think to myself, *with all the barreling trains that pass by.*

"How late did Johnny say he'd be, Arch?"

"He didn't. . . . Said he had to talk to the coach about something."

"Crap. Do you think he's gonna tell Credos what we're doing? Rat on us?"

"Nah, that's not Johnny's style. I just hope he didn't screw up again. The coach has been keeping a tight eye on him—almost stalkin' 'im."

Junior said he and Jamal saw the stash. . . . Maybe Johnny did, too.

I kick at the dirt. "What happened that day . . . the day Junior was busted? It took Junior by surprise, right?"

"Yeah. The cops cuffed him. He was crying out, *'It's not mine, I promise! The stuff ain't mine!'*"

"How was the coach acting while this went on?"

Archie chews on a blade of grass. "Now that I'm thinkin' about it . . . he just kinda stood there, his arms folded. Didn't say much."

"Don't you think that's a little odd?"

"I dunno. I try not to think about it . . . about Junior. It messes with my head when I go there." He looks away, down the tracks, and mumbles, "Sometimes makes me want to use again."

The sun starts to drop, casting the sky in an orangeish light—scratchy-looking, like a clump of Play-Doh, when you mix the red with the yellow and forget to put the lid back on. "What was it—your drug of choice, Archie?"

He spits out a fleck of grass. "Coke. Don't much dig the downer feel. I need to be up. You? Did you use?" His cheeks are now flushed, probably with the rush of the memory.

I explode with a deep, guttural laugh. "Uh, yeah. I sure did. But I liked the smorgasbord—the whole enchilada." Big exhale. "Needed to escape . . . didn't care how—had to get outta myself, outta my head."

"I know what you mean." He blows through his lips. Looks around. "I don't know where Johnny is, but we might as well do our thing, before it gets too dark. You up for this?"

"Here? We're kind of out in the open." I *so* don't want Detective Cole to come squealing up in his Batmobile. Even if this isn't his district, he'd find a way, his face all greasy with KFC or Domino's pizza, to arrest me again . . . the last thing I need. That would seal the deal with Sergeant Daniels never wanting to work with me—never wanting to see me again.

Archie stands, hitches up his jeans. "No, not here. We're going to the Tridge, like I told ya. We'll train-bomb later, if we have time. You down with that?"

"Down, dude."

My phone buzzes in my back pocket. I take a peek. *Daniels.* I don't answer.

"Who's that?"

"No one."

Archie tightens the straps on his backpack as we get to the entrance of the Tridge: a massive three-way wooden footbridge that spans the Huron River, connecting Depot Town, Frog Island Park, and Riverside Park. The heavily trafficked Cross Street bridge hovers above—a bridge that runs right by the courthouse.

"Hey, Arch. I don't see any tags anywhere on the Tridge."

"Yeah, they're keeping it clean. Now that it's all lit up, it's hard to hit. The secret's underneath."

"Underneath?"

He jogs across the wooden slats to where the three arms connect—waves me over. "Pull down your ski mask and put this on." He tosses me a flashlight headband.

"Cool." I strap it on.

"It's going to get dark under there."

"Under where?" I ask through the itchy knit of the mask.

He points at the underside of the bridge above. "Only rule? Don't fall. If you do, you'll end up in the water. It won't kill you—it's pretty shallow, but the muck and weeds will take you down, fast." He hoots. "I can't swim, and I don't wanna have to jump in after you."

"You're friggin' kidding me, right? We're going to tag the bottom of the Cross Street bridge?"

"Yup." He hops on the outside of the wooden railing as if he's on a balance beam, reaches for the support girder on the bridge above, and hoists himself up, lifts his legs, wraps them around a chunky box beam, then pulls his body up and around. He sits straight up, straddling the beam, like he mounted a horse five feet above me. "You got that?"

"Could you do it again? But this time in slow motion?"

He snickers. "It's not that hard. And once you're here—if you make it this far—you're all set. It's a piece of cake after this. There's a sizeable ledge, and scaffolding that spans the length of the bridge. Don't worry. I'm here to spot you."

I clamber up onto the railing, crouch, holding on tightly with my hands, and make the mistake of looking down. The water is about twenty feet below; even though we don't have them in Michigan, I think I spot an alligator swimming down-stream. It could be a crocodile, but I've never known the difference, and it really doesn't matter—they'd both eat me.

I raise my arms super fast in the air, grab the girder, and then stand on my tiptoes, allowing me to hug the hard metal edges of the beam—hanging on for dear life.

"That's it." Archie cheers me on. "Now you just have to get your legs up and around."

I close my eyes, and drop my legs, dangle them one at a time, pulling hard with my upper body, hoping, praying, that the biceps I've never asked much from in my life will somehow do me a solid and kick in. I struggle to get my right foot around the beam.

"Almost there," Archie says. "Then hoist the other one up to meet it."

With a grunt, my leg somehow makes contact with the other foot, and I find myself hanging upside down. "Okay, now what?" I ask, out of breath.

"Look up." He shines a heavy-duty flashlight above our heads and illuminates intricate, bold-colored graffiti saturating the cast concrete of the bridge in both directions, like an "out-of-this world," colorful, inspiring mural that would put that neo-expressionism chapter in my art book to shame.

All of a sudden I think of my mom and wish she were here with me. She'd get this, my mom. She would. A warm, fuzzy feeling whooshes over me, like how the tree in my front yard makes me feel—grounded, safe—even though I'm dangling twenty feet over a river. "You were right, Arch; it's friggin' beautiful."

"Told ya." He smiles with his voice. "But you gotta pull yourself up now so we can do our thing and add to it."

I suck in my tummy, flex my legs, pull with my arms, try to scramble up and around the beam—but nope, doesn't happen. I try again, grunting, hoping the sound effects will somehow flip me.

"Lemme help you."

I have no choice but to let him. It's either that, falling, or living my life as a bat, upside down under a bridge.

He reaches down, wrapping his arm around my waist, brushing slightly across my unbound breasts, *oh god*, and helps me twist around till I'm upright. I calm my breath, sitting across from him, and see his laughing eyes behind the woolen mask.

"What?"

"Nice rack you got there, *boy*." He slaps his thigh. "Like you really thought you were foolin' anyone? I knew from day one."

I bunch the ski mask up on my forehead. "Holy crap, how?"

"Well, for one, you left your tampon wrapper in the stall."

Do I jump now?

"And you smell too good to be a guy."

"I can't believe you didn't say anything."

"I wanted to see how far you'd go. Shit, Reyna thinks you're all about the bi scene. We were all making bets. But I don't know; I don't pick up on that."

"What d'you pick up on, then?"

He pulls off the hat and clears his throat. "I'd like to see you with chick clothes on. . . . Betcha you're cute, Boy."

"The name's Bea. B-E-A. Short for Beatrice."

"Nice to meet ya, Bea—short for Beatrice." He high-fives me, almost pushing me off the beam and into the water.

"Whoa . . ."

He takes hold of my shoulders, steadying me.

I pull the mask back down and never want to take it off again. "I am so humiliated."

"Why the charade? What's your story?"

I shrug. "The coach just assumed I was a guy, and there's no way I was going to argue with him."

Archie laughs. "Good call."

"Like I said, I'm wandering. The 'rents are splitting up; all the peeps I know and love are skipping town, leaving me." *Unfortunately the truth.*

"I know how you feel. Same thing happened to me a few years back. That's why I love doin' my art; it's cathartic as hell, man." He shines the light to his right. "There's some virgin space over there. Good place to throw some paint, get it all out." He scrambles onto the iron ledge and crawls on his hands and knees across the scaffolding. I follow—not as confident, but manage to stay above the water.

Archie sits on his butt and looks up. "Ta-da. Our palate. Lie down, get yourself comfortable. Mark your territory. But don't bite no one."

"What?" I laugh to myself, remembering the *biter* reference with Daniels.

"Don't steal anyone's shit. You don't want war."

Archie unzips his backpack and pulls out a can of spray paint. A plastic baggie filled with white powder falls out. He quickly snatches it up and shoves it back in the pack like it didn't happen.

Shit . . . he said he wasn't using anymore.

He tosses over the paint. "Tag your signature . . . somethin' original."

"Sure, I guess I can do that." I pull off my Pokémon backpack, strap it on the front of my belly, and lie down on my back. I switch on the forehead flashlight, and take note of a rather large gap between the support beams a foot to my right, the wake of the river flickering underneath. A truck rumbles above, sounding like a barreling freight train; the whole bridge vibrates. "This is gnarly up here, Arch," I yell out. "This must've been how Michelangelo felt painting the ceiling of the Sistine Chapel, right?"

"I think I'm more like Leonardo da Vinci," he calls out.

"What do you mean?" I look over at him through the slits of my mask.

"Da Vinci wrote backward." He shakes his can of paint, pops off the cap, and sprays out *Y-P-S-I.*

"That's your signature, Arch? Ypsi? Short for Ypsilanti?"

"Nah . . . that's too lame. Read it backward. I-S-P-Y. I spy. Clever, huh? Junior came up with it. Shit, we had some good times under here."

My body goes numb. *It's not the coach's tat that Junior was thinking about; it's Archie's tag. And he's lying about being clean; he's still doing blow. Holy fuck . . . Could Archie be the OG, the kingpin?* I fumble my phone out of my back pocket.

"Hey, Bea. Why aren't you spraying?" Archie crouches now, his arms on his knees.

"I dunno. I'm feeling a little headache coming on. I get them sometimes." I roll to my side, and punch in Sergeant Daniels's number, press the speaker button—muffle the rings under my sweatshirt as I fake a few coughs and then talk loudly toward the phone. "I think that maybe my hat's too tight. I'm going to turn it around on my head!" I yell.

Archie starts crawling toward me like a crab. "What? What are you talking about?"

I sit up, pull the phone out from under my sweatshirt, and hear the sergeant's voice; Archie hears his voice, too, on speaker, as he shouts, *"BEA! WHERE ARE YOU?"*

"Who are you talking to?" he hisses.

I scream into the phone. "The usual place, now!"

Archie leaps toward me. I tuck my arms around the back-pack, covering my face, and roll to the right, falling off the edge of the bridge, down, down, down, splashing hard into the water.

I scrape the jagged, rocky bottom of the river—gurgling. I struggle to lift my head, take a breath, and hear a second splash. I immediately feel him grab my right ankle, pulling me back under the water. I try to kick his hand away with my other foot, but he grabs it tighter and pulls me toward him.

I snag a slimy, moss-green rock buried in the muddy bottom, twist my torso around, turning onto my back, and crash the rock into Archie's hand, and my own shin.

He howls, releases my leg, and our blood mingles around like smoke in the gray-green hazy water. His tiger-yellow eyes blaze as he powers forward—his body stopping suddenly in a tangle of seaweed. Archie struggles, contorts his face, growls, resembling the monster reptile I thought I saw earlier. He yells, "You're a narc, aren't you? That's what this is all about."

"No, I'm not, Archie! I'm not a narc. I don't care about you carrying. I really, really don't."

"I'm going to fuckin' kill you." He lurches toward me.

I thrash toward the riverbank, pulling off my soaked sweatshirt. I flip my backpack on my back, thanking the foam-filled picture of Pikachu for saving my face from crashing into the rocks, and scramble up onto the shore. I feel the blood oozing out of my knee and my shin—the warmth of it. Numbness replaced with pain, strangely giving me strength, and I kick into high gear.

Archie is screaming maybe fifteen feet behind me. I run along the mucky shore, splashing through the water. A mother goose and her babies flap their feathers, quack, yell at me— totally flustered and pissed off, as I run upstream. The weedy reeds wrap around my ankles; I trip over a rock, get another mouthful of silt, cough, spit it out, and keep on running, making my way to the footbridge ahead that will take me to the courthouse.

Archie's splashing gets closer; I hear his heavy breathing; and then suddenly a blast—a high-pitch *whirring*—shoots past my right ear, slams, and shatters into the trunk of a young maple five feet from my head.

Fuck. He has a gun.

I spot a concrete culvert to my right and duck inside. Another blast ricochets off the cement. I flinch. My ears ring. I have nowhere else to go, so I crouch and move deeper into the concrete passageway—the flashlight still strapped to my head, shining in the darkness. I bend over; my hands scrape along the side, guide me, help catapult me through the tunnel. Then I hear Archie's breath echo off the walls and run a little faster, trying to keep my footing on the slimy, slick cement.

The ceiling of the tunnel gets lower and narrower, and I fall to my knees and crawl through inches of muck. The back of my head rubs against the top. The water starts to rise—gets higher, up to my waist now, as the tunnel seems to veer off to the left and slant down. *Under the river. The tunnel is taking me under the Huron.* The water is now up to my nose.

I can't turn back. There has to be an end; the tunnel has to lead to somewhere—the river isn't that wide. I know it can't be that far. Please, don't let it be that far.

I stretch my legs out behind me, take a deep breath, and dunk my head, shoot my arms out in front of my body, and paddle my feet as fast as I can in the tight space. The water is dark gray, thick, and stinks, like I'm sludging through a vat of rancid Jell-O. I blink my eyes open and close, praying for the end to be in sight; they sting, and my lungs start to burn. My headache has morphed into dizziness, and I'm feeling as if I might pass out, when something swims alongside my body.

I scream a silent underwater scream as a crayfish the size of a five-pound lobster surges ahead of me. *Oh my god, I gotta get the fuck outta here.* I see a hint of a light ahead in the wake of the crustacean, kick my feet with everything I have. Suddenly my hand touches a dry stone surface up above my head. I slap my other hand on what feels like a rocky shelf, pull my torso up and out of the water, and gulp the stagnant air as if I were in the crisp altitude of the Alps. The water, diverted, follows the channel, rushes down, off me, past me. I look behind; there's no sign of Archie. Hopefully, he didn't follow; he said he couldn't swim.

The flashlight still strapped to my head flickers on and off, illuminating a stone corridor. I trudge my soaked, battered body ahead and limp past hollowed, empty cubbies, like cells. *This must be the old jail . . . I'm below the courthouse!* The walls are covered with layers and layers of angry graffiti, and the words, the image of Archie's tag, *I spy,* floods my head. *I spy you, Bea. I see you. This is where you belong—where you deserve to be . . . down here in this hole.* My stomach tightens; my heart flutters—just like it did in the holding cell at the police station.

I hear something behind me, scuffling—squeaking. I slowly turn and see a huge raccoon sitting, fingering, clawing at something . . . probably the crayfish. Its eyes meet the shine of the light on my forehead, and it peers at me like I'm dessert or something. It hisses with its foul-smelling breath. I answer with a scream, scaring it as it scampers away, and up a stairway. *The stairs! The stairs to the courthouse!*

I follow the vermin, picking up speed—taking the stairs two at a time. I duck under the rusted chain, run across the room, and throw my body against the plywood, crawl through the window, and fall onto the damp, cold ground.

The moon is full, bright; the sky clear; and the constellations are weighty, hanging in the sky like the mobile in Mr. Pogen's Sea of Tranquility class. Breathing hard, I pull my waterlogged cell out of my pocket. It's dead. I roll up the leg of my jeans. My knee has totally opened up; the shin below is bleeding. I get out the bandana from the drenched backpack, mop up the blood, and tie it tightly around my leg, praying that infection hasn't set in yet, and then hobble around the side of the building toward the front through dense, prickly bushes. Sergeant Daniels should have made it here by now. The branches on the other side of the building rustle. "Dan? Is that you?" I whisper. *Please be you.*

He grabs me from behind. His left hand covers my mouth. The barrel of the gun juts up against my ribs.

And I bite him . . . *hard.*

"Ouch, shit." Archie throws me to the ground. He checks out his hand, sucks at the wound. I'm on my butt, looking up into the whites of his eyes shining brightly in the moonlight. His clothes are soaked and ripped. Blood drips from the ragged gash on his right forearm. Seaweed dangles in his long hair, and his Glock now points directly at my head.

I cower, cover my face, and wait for the blast.

"Drop the gun." I hear Sergeant Daniels's voice behind me. I turn. He stands at the side of the building with his arms straight out, his weapon pointed at Archie, flashing his badge with his left hand. "Put the gun down. Now!" he orders.

Archie flinches; his hands are shaking. He looks at the sergeant and then back at me—the gun staring at my face. "Don't no one make a move, or the bitch is dead."

Daniels focuses steadily on his target. "Bea, do what he says. Don't budge."

I'm suddenly freezing cold and start to shiver—out of control; then I see movement in the woods behind Archie. The homeless man steps out from the dark gully. "Hey, what's going on? What are you doing to her?" he yells, and starts toward us.

"Watch out! He has a gun!" I shout out, my teeth chattering.

Everything speeds up in slow motion. Archie swings around. The homeless guy ducks, runs back into the thicket. I rush toward Archie as he fires, charge into his legs, pushing us both down on the ground. The bullet violently skids across the dirt, uprooting the foliage in its path.

"Bea! Roll to your right!" Daniels yells.

I do. Archie starts to swing his gun around at Daniels when the sergeant fires, hitting him in the right shoulder, forcing his firearm to fall from his hand.

Archie wails, thrashes around on the ground, holding his wound. "You shot me. . . . You fucking hit me!"

Sergeant Daniels holsters his weapon, runs up, flips Archie on his belly, and cuffs his wrists behind his back. He starts reading him his Miranda rights, then calls for help. All the time Archie's blubbering, rolling around, and crying like a baby.

Daniels pulls me into his chest and drapes his jacket over my shoulders. "It's okay. You're going to be okay."

I hear his voice as if I'm back in the tunnel—it's muffled, distant. I know his arm is around me, but I don't feel it. He lifts my chin. His eyes, shots of fire, burn through me. His lips move like an animation film, flipping through one cell, one image at a time. But I don't hear what he's saying. I bury my head back into his chest and listen for it: the *ba-dump*, *ba-dump*, *ba-dump* of his heart. I hang on to the sound, the beat, the rhythm. My breath falls in step, in time with the pounding, and I feel as if I am slowly rising back to the surface . . . to what? To where? "Junior . . ." I nod my head fast. "I have to get to him. Let him know I figured it out . . . that we got Archie." My voice sounds like it's coming from inside a tin can.

"You can't, Bea. You can't. He died. A couple hours ago. I tried to get ahold of you."

"Oh, fuck, Junior . . ." Archie, hearing this . . . moans.

I pull away from the sergeant. "What? He can't be dead. That's not supposed to happen." And then I barrel over to Archie, still lying on the ground on his stomach. I throw myself at him and start beating his back. "He died!" I scream. "Why did you do it?"

"I didn't wanna have to shoot 'im. He was my bro. I thought he woulda stayed quiet—wouldn't have ratted on me," he cries.

Daniels pulls me off him. "Bea, stop."

"He wasn't the rat, Archie. I was!"

"What the fuck?" Archie looks back at me, half of his face wedged in the dirt.

"I told the cops." I sob.

"You fuckin' snitch." Archie spits onto the ground. "Then *you* killed him, not me."

Sirens wail in the distance—getting closer. I break away from Daniels and run down the hill.

"Bea, no, come back!"

I cross the footbridge, run to my car parked at the station. My legs fly, barely touching the ground. I dig in my backpack for my keys, turn on the engine, pull away, and start driving to who-the-hell-knows-where-ville.

3 minutes

Secrets. *Lies.* They smother. But the truth—sometimes the truth is worse. It kills. Leaves blood on your hands.

I eventually had to stop for gas in some hick town just south of Brighton. I used the restroom—totally gross—took off my drenched T-shirt, the sopped face mask, the ratted, torn jeans, and stuffed them in the trash. Of course the soap dispenser was empty, so I doused myself, saturated my wounds with the whole bottle of hand sanitizer that Willa thoughtfully gave me last week. I rinsed and wrung out the blood-soaked bandana, scrubbed my face with it, my pits, everywhere . . . and wrapped my knee and shin with a thick roll of toilet paper.

After riffling through stuff on the backseat, I found a large navy V-neck sweater of Wendell's, and the smell of vanilla coffee beans wafted over me—a step up from rotting seaweed, for sure. I tugged the tie-dyed maxi skirt up over my hips, laced my high-tops, and finished the look with Dan Daniels's jacket.

The woodsy eucalyptus scent trumped the vanilla beans, and of course, beat up, bloodied, exhausted, and lost, my tummy still did the flip-flop thing.

I picked up a bag of salted peanuts, a couple candy bars, and a few bottles of water from a convenience store, and I've been driving north on the road for hours now—driving fast in the middle of nowhere—toward nothing—blindly. Not wanting to see, not wanting to be seen.

The clock on my dashboard says it's midnight—*happy birthday, me.* I am eighteen, going on . . . life—an adult. I can head anywhere I want. Do anything I want. Be anyone I want. I have everything I need in the car—could get jobs along the way, flip burgers, maybe earn my GED, learn the tat trade, and eventually open my own shop . . . in northern Michigan. Yeah, sure, like that'll ever happen.

Fuck it. I need a sign—something—telling me *where* to go, *what* to do, *who* to be. A streetlight shines ahead at an intersection. I step hard on the accelerator, speeding to get through fast, not wanting the light in my eyes.

Holy crap. What is that?

I slam on the brakes . . . come to a dead stop, catch my breath, and there it sits, in the middle of the intersection. A dog.

I step out of my car. My knees (what's left of them) buckle a little. I shake my legs and march over. "What were you thinking? Sitting there, in the middle of the road, huh? I almost hit you."

He yawns.

"Oh, right. It doesn't mean anything to you . . . scaring the hell out of me like that."

I hear a car in the distance and see the blurry lights approaching.

"Okay, boy, if that's what you are, I need you to come with me now. Do you hear me? NOW."

He doesn't budge.

I bend down, reach out, and the dog growls. "You don't understand; it's not safe here. . . . I can't help you if you don't move."

The car gets closer.

"God dammit. You can't just sit there frozen, like you don't give a shit. Come, please . . . come." I turn, start walking away, hoping he will follow me. He doesn't. "Ugh. Fine. I don't care if you bite me. But no way I'm going to let you get hit by that car. No friggin' way."

I reach down, and the dog now places its paw in my hand, as if to shake. "We don't have time for that." I scoop him up and jog to the side of the road, just as the car whizzes by. He licks my nose—I can't help but laugh.

"That was really stupid, what you did. Do you understand? You could have been killed."

The dog looks at me straight in the eyes—his scruffy black head cocks to the right as he sighs, lying limply in my arms. I put him on the ground, and he shakes out his fur, starting with his head, all the way down to his tail. Then he saunters past me, jumps in the driver's seat, and gazes out the front window.

I throw my arms up and walk to the car. "Okay, fine, move over." He does—to the passenger seat—and I join him in the car.

He looks straight out the front window at the empty road and makes a whiny noise.

"My thoughts exactly."

"You have a name?" I turn the ropy, dirty beige collar on his neck, searching for an ID tag. "You lost? No home?"

His stomach growls.

I rummage around the backseat, open the pizza box, and grab a cardboard-stiff slice of pepperoni and cheese. "I have no idea how old this is." I offer it to the dog. He bows his wiry head as if to say thanks and gently bites the slice, pulling it out of my hand. "Glad to see you're not picky." I pour some water into an empty Styrofoam coffee cup and join him in taking a few gulps myself from the bottle.

He laps it up, splashing it around the front seat, all over the dash, and all over me. Then he sneezes.

"Hah. Allergies. I understand." I wipe the fur around his face with the red bandana and wrap it around his neck. "Sorry it's wet, but it looks nice on you."

His ears perk up on his head, forming fuzzy triangles, and then one flops down. His wet nose shines in the dark. His eyes wide, perfect circles, like two black buttons, pools of dark, wet ink, just like . . .

A clump of emotion lodges in the middle of my throat. "Junior. You like that name?"

He stretches out his front paws, lying on the seat.

I lean down and hug him. "We're going to be okay," I say into his fur. "We'll figure it out, right?" I sit up, swallow, un-lodging the clump from my throat.

I start the car, make a U-turn. I take note of the time: eleven minutes into my eighteenth birthday, and scan the empty road ahead.

"So, where to now, Junior?"

Woof.

My Junior
2000–2012

I miss you so.

AUTHOR'S NOTE

The history behind Depot Town in Ypsilanti fascinated me. The tunnels, for various reasons and purposes, do indeed exist under Ypsilanti and Ann Arbor, as does the courthouse and the "Tridge." I did, however, invoke narrative license with locations and descriptions.

To learn more about Depot Town, please check out:
http://en.wikipedia.org/wiki/Depot_Town

ACKNOWLEDGMENTS

They say write what you know. *I* say write what you don't know, use your imagination, research, pry, and then stalk people. Eventually someone caves and shares their expertise, a glimpse through a cracked door into their world. Some of the brave souls were:

Manny Jimenez: for sharing your life story with me. You truly are a guardian angel for many, and now I'm so fortunate to be on that list. You inspired me and gave me the courage to write about a world I knew nothing about.

Mills McIlroy: for retelling your inspiring "Shawshank" cross-country experience through the tunnels—and most important, for living through it!

Dawn Roberts-Mark: for painstakingly going through the curl-scale talks with me with a fine-tooth comb (pun intended).

To the men in uniform: Retired Chicago Police Department Homicide Detective and former Investigator for the Office of the Illinois Attorney General, Gregory Baiocchi; Retired Detroit Arson Lieutenant/Investigator, Maurice Dewey; and Executive Petty Officer, US Coast Guard, Allen Hosford. Your advice and expertise were invaluable.

You can take the girl out of Michigan, but never take Michigan out of the girl, and I am indebted to my Michigander partners in crime: my mom; sisters Janey and Monica, David Guilbert, Gary and Max McIlroy, Jennifer Carolynn, and Fred Dewey. Big hugs for driving me around the 'hood, sharing your Ann Arbor/Ypsilanti experiences, and answering my incessant texts and calls.

My bff Susan: you've shored me up when I was consumed by self-doubt. Kicked me in the butt when I wanted to give up. Laughed at me when I needed "to get over it." Cried with me when I couldn't. Thank you. (And a virtual fist bump goes to Lily for her "teen-speak" info line.)

My amazing Amazonian team: Larry, Amy, Marilyn, Timoney, Deborah, Erick, Katrina, Ariel, and Tim . . . your support and encouragement have been phenomenal. Thanks also to Sammy Yuen and Susan Gerber for the killer cover and book design. I am so grateful to each and every one of you, and feel as if you are family.

Lisa Gallagher, my agent: I don't know of another person that works as hard and wears as many hats as you. You continue to awe me with your fast-as-lightning reads, spot-on, inspiring editorial eye, wicked sense of humor, and ability and willingness to talk me through the "crazy-insecure-as-hell" periods.

And, always, the triangle of love that surrounds me—my husband, daughter, and son. I love you.

ABOUT THE AUTHOR

Olivia Samms is the author of the Bea Catcher Chronicles. *Sketchy*, her debut novel and the first in the series, received a starred review in *Publishers Weekly*. Olivia lives with her husband and two children in Los Angeles, where she is working on the next book in the Bea Catcher Chronicles.

Learn more: www.oliviasamms.com